Jed Chance:

Ride

For

Justice

Book One in the Jed Chance Series

Arthur Mendenhall

Cover layout and interior pages
layout by Capri Porter.

Printed in the United States of America

ISBN: 978-0-9972523-7-8

Published by
Legacies & Memories
St. Augustine, Florida

(888) 862-2754
www.LegaciesandMemoriesPublishing.com

Contact the Author
E-mail: JedChance@yahoo.com

Dedication

First, this work is dedicated to my wife, Becky. She is the inspiration for all good things in my life.

Second, this is dedicated to our friends, Greg and Chrisanne Street. It was their encouragement that got me to finish writing this story.

A Note from the Author

I have included in this work of fiction some actual people who lived at the time and in the places mentioned in the book. All the places mentioned – Dallas, Plano, Lampasas and Leon Creek – and others are, of course, actual places in Texas. Any mistakes as to time, place or people are mine and mine alone.

Here are a few other interesting points:

King and Kenedy Ranch mentioned in chapter one was a true ranch and the men did eventually divide their ranch, and Kenedy started a new ranch that grew to approximately 200,000 acres.

Camp Street in 1873 was a rough and tumble area and Doc's saloon did exist. It was one of the tamest drinking establishments on the street.

The "Kerr and Gruber Bank" was in operation in Dallas in 1873, but I do not think it was in as close proximity to the railroad yard as I have placed it in this work.

Sheriff James Barkley was in office in 1873 and Bev and Tom Scott were his deputies.

Belle Starr was stealing horses and cattle from

ranchers around Dallas in 1873.

Clint and Jesse Padgitt were saddle makers in Dallas in 1873.

"Sanger's" store was in operation in 1873 and was a thriving business in Dallas for many years after.

Mart Howell and his brothers were true bad men of the old west. They did, in fact, kill the sheriff of Lampasas and a couple of months later, four state police officers in Jerry's saloon as mentioned in this work. They fled to Lincoln County, New Mexico, and resided there for a while before returning to Lampasas. Mart and his gang killed many Hispanic people just because they were who they were.

I hope the reader will allow me some license in such things as time and distance. I have tried to be true to the accepted fact that a good rider on a good horse could travel about fifty miles a day. I think that's on a really good day, traveling light and over relatively smooth ground. Jed, Craig and other characters in this book do not cover that much ground in a day.

I hope you enjoy reading the first of Jed's adventures.

Jed Chance:
Ride
For
Justice

Chapter 1

Ruth Adams is tired. The kind of tired that is worn like a heavy coat, it goes to the bones and just never seems to leave. She has been tired for a long time. A blonde woman of thin build and only twenty-nine, she feels like her years number a hundred. Once considered pretty by anyone's standards, she now was hardened, and worn. Texas in 1873 did that to a woman when trying to scratch out a living on a hardscrabble ranch. She stood on the broken-down porch of the two-room ranch house she shared with her man, Craig Mullins, and a boy, Jeff, on a dry, dusty patch of land they called a horse ranch. It was that in name only. They were in the ranch yard working on the rusty water pump trying to get the unyielding beast of a contraption to put forth some of its precious liquid. It had been two days of work and still nothing.

Something caused her to look up and toward the southwest, across the gently waving buffalo grass. In the distance, she saw a dot. Heat waves made the dark dot rise and fall. She returned her focus to the work Craig and Jeff were doing, but after a few minutes, she shielded her eyes and looked again toward the dot that now had taken the shape of a man on horseback, headed for the ranch.

"Craig, Jeff, rider coming—coming from the southwest."

Craig Mullins, a man of dark hair and medium build and mustache stood and looked in the direction of the rider.

"Yep, see him. He'll be here in ten or so minutes." Craig turned to Jeff, a skinny, blonde boy with a freckled face and big brown eyes of eleven or so in years that had taken up with him and Ruth a few years back and told him, "Jeff, head over to the barn, take up the pitchfork and hide inside. Ruth, baby, step inside and hand me my Sharps. We'll just sit here and wait on 'em. I need a break from this bitch of broken down metal anyway."

"Craig, you got two shells for that old rifle and the stock might not stay on if you fired it once."

"The stranger won't know that Ruth, so just hand it to me and have a sit on the porch, there by the door, 'case you need to duck inside."

Ruth reached inside the door and grabbed the old '51 Sharps and handed it over to Craig and then sat on the end of the porch bench, right by the front door. Craig sat on the steps, Sharps across his legs. He leaned against the porch post and watched and waited.

As the figure drew closer, Craig mused, mostly to himself, "Ummm, sits his horse like a cavalryman. He sits like him but... couldn't be." Then, "Damn my eyes, could it be?"

Ruth could sense growing tension in Craig as he stood up and began a nervous light rocking, left to right, left to right.

Ruth saw that man was now at the edge of the yard. He was a big, rawboned man, 6'4", maybe a might taller, and well over two hundred pounds. A full-grown man, wearing an old slouch hat pulled low that blocked his face from her view, tattered and torn canvas pants, worn down low heeled boots, a faded and sweat stained shirt that once might have been blue but all color had long since been washed out by sun and rain. Ruth could see a sidearm sticking out butt first on his left side. He was a big man with big, rough hands; a man who just by his look, you knew would truck no nonsense.

His horse was played out. He had been played out for a year or two by the looks of it and was worn thin to the bone. Hip and rib bones stood out in stark relief to its dirty, pale coat. Head drooping, it was barely shuffling along.

The stranger raised his head and revealed blue eyes and a blonde mustache adorning a weathered face that was not totally unpleasing to the eye except for the scar that ran from his right temple down his face to the corner of his lip and stood out in sharp contrast to the rest of his wind and sunburned face. His long, blonde hair was pulled back and tied with a rawhide thong. The blue eyes were lively and alert and seemed to be looking everywhere at once. His big hands held the reins loose between his fingers.

Ruth stood up as Craig said, "Been awhile, Jed!"

"Yea," the stranger uttered in a low, quiet voice, "I got held up a time or two."

"Uh, think you was held up for 'bout seven years by my figuring!" replied Craig, a smile spreading across his face.

"Best I could do was now," sighed the big man.

The man's eyes took in the dilapidated old

spread as Craig came off the porch and he said, "Well, I see I got here just in time to take part in the prosperity you all are enjoying."

Craig laughed and stuck out his hand as the stranger slowly dismounted and turned to Craig. Ignoring the outstretched hand, he grabbed Craig in a bear hug and both men were laughing and yelling, and dust flew from both their clothes as they smiled big smiles and pounded each other on the back.

Ruth took all this in with open mouth surprise, "Is this him? Is this Jed Chance?"

"Yep, his own self! Jedediah Abraham Chance," said Craig.

Turning to Ruth and tipping his old hat, the big man said, "Yes, mama, that would be me."

"Damn boy!" said Craig, "Just damn!"

"Good to see you too old friend! Now, is the man you got sitting in the barn a friend or do I have cause to worry?"

"Oh, yea, I forgot. Jeff! Jeff, get over here! It's OK. It's my friend from the war, Jed Chance. Get on over here!"

"See you still have it, Jed. Eyes in the back of your head, and maybe sides too!" grinned Craig.

Jed smiled, "Just trying to stay alive."

"Yes Ruth, this is Cap'n Jed Chance, late of the Confederate States of America, Army of Northern Virginia and one of old Andrew Jackson's favorites and not a man to be trifled with."

"You sure it's him?" shouted Jeff as his bare feet kicked up puffs of dust as he trotted over from the barn.

"'Course I'm sure. I served with him for 'bout the whole war! Covering his ass and saving his worthless life."

"Hey, now, I think we both did a little ass-covering and life-saving for each other."

"Yes, my friend, that surely is true. Jed, this here is my woman, Ruth, and the boy here is, Jeff."

"Hello, Ruth," Chance said as he tipped his hat to her, then to the boy, "Howdy, Jeff."

"Hey, Cap'n Chance, boy it's sure nice to meet you. Wow! You sure are big as Craig said, maybe bigger! Craig here has told me so much about you and the dust-ups you and he had during the war," said Jeff as he grinned at Chance.

"Just a civilian now, Jeff, not a Captain anymore; those days are long gone."

Ruth stepped off the porch and took Jed's big

hand, "Nice to finally meet you, Jed. Looks like you showed up at a bad time, the cupboard is nigh on to empty."

Jed smiled and moved to his saddle, reached over and fetched a small pouch from his saddlebag and removed from the other side of his saddle two fat jackrabbits already cleaned and gutted. "Well, I got a little coffee in this here bag and some rabbit ready for frying and I surely don't mind sharing."

"Well, it'll be cowboy coffee, fry bread and rabbit for all tonight!" said Ruth.

"And while we are eating, Jed can tell us why it took so long for him to get here," said Craig.

Responded Jed, "And you can tell me why you don't have a hundred or so head of prime horseflesh running around this here ranch!"

Craig smiled and they all went to wash up.

Chapter 2

During their meal, Jed related to everyone how he had moved west from New Orleans into south Texas seeking work and money to help with the stocking of the ranch with horses that he and Craig had planned on. It was reconstruction times and things were tough especially for the men who had worn the uniform of the confederacy and jobs weren't easy to come by. In Medallion, Galveston, and Houston, Jed was able to get a job as a lawman. After several years of that life, he moved on to various ranches learning the cattle trade and driving cattle to the Montana gold mines, New Mexico Indian reservations, and the Kansas trail heads.

"I wandered into Brownsville and later took up a job at the Santa Gertrudis Ranch," related Jed. "And, well, then there was a girl..."

"Should 'a known that was the holdup," said Craig.

"She was special Craig. She was a pretty little

16

thing teaching school there on the ranch to the little ones. I got some education from her, too."

"Bet you did!" said a grinning Jeff.

"Hush, Jeff! Mind your elders!" said Ruth.

"Well, we got married and then, well, a year or so later she died. It was some lung thing. The doctor could do nothing for her," said Jed, with memories of his late wife filling his mind as he gazed out into the night.

"Santa Gertrudis, isn't that the big King and Kenedy's ranch?" asked Craig.

"Yea, it was, but they split the blanket on it and Mr. Kenedy took a new ranch, Los Laurels, just outside of Corpus Christi. I moved on with Kenedy. Big ranch it is. I bet it's thousands of acres now. Anyway, ranch got too big for me, and I was feeling guilty about not showing up here, so I fetched up my gear and headed over to see if I could locate you. 'Bout a week ago I ran into a group of Comanche and was lucky to get out with my hair. Lost everything to them boys, 'cept my pack horse and this old hide out Colt I had," Jed said as he patted the worn grip of his pistol.

They talked on for a while longer, then. "Mr. Chance" said Jeff, "Craig done told me 'bout all your scrapes and battles and men you kil't in the war. Tell me some stories! Tell me 'bout a good killing!"

Chance's eyes became flint hard as he turned toward the boy. "No such thing as a good killing, Jeff. It's all just killing. Man needs it you do it, simple as that. Please, don't ask no more about it."

Ruth sensed Chance's irritation at the question. "The boy didn't mean no harm, Jed. Just curious I guess. Let's — let's all turn in, it's getting late. Jeff, head on over to the barn and Jed, I'm guessing you'll be bedding down there, too."

"Yes, mama, that will be fine with me. Surely Jeff will make a good bunkmate," said Jed as he tousled Jeff's hair.

Ruth and Jeff rose, and Jeff headed to the barn and Ruth got busy cleaning up the supper dishes.

"Craig, we gon'a work on that pump in the morning?" asked Chance.

"No need. Damn things busted. I need a new one but no money for it."

"Let's go to Dallas in the morning, see if we can scare up some work, make some money and get it done," said Chance.

"Ok, let's do that. I been thinking I needed to do

something like that and with you here, well, let's do it."

The old friends sat in silence for a few minutes, finishing their coffee, and then Jed said, "Going to turn in now but how 'bout stepping outside a quick minute with me."

The two men stepped out on the porch. Jed turned to his friend and said, "Pard, riding in, I could see horse tracks, day or day and a half old, well-shod mounts of ten to maybe twelve men. Noticed they came into your yard and I am pretty sure they lead on out toward Dallas."

Craig looked at his friend, cleared his throat, and said, "Yea, yea, you know a few of 'em, too. They came in yesterday morning, early. Jeff and Ruth were fetching water from the Trinity, so they didn't see 'em. It was Sam Rogers, his brothers, Randy and Bob, and eight or nine hard cases. Some of the boys from the war we served with and some I ain't ever seen before."

"How'd they know you was here?"

"I don't rightly know. I guess I talked about the ranch to some of 'em way back in the war."

"What'd they want?"

"Think they are up to no good. Sam asked me to ride with them to Dallas, said they were looking for some traveling money. I don't think he was planning to work for it."

Chance nodded and leaned against the porch post. "That Sam and his brothers was a bad lot when we served with 'em and surely, they haven't changed any. Best we both steer a wide path around them if we run onto them."

"Sam asked if I knew where you were. He's hated you ever since you busted his head and got him knocked down in rank from Captain to private by General Lee."

"Craig, he raped and killed that woman! She was a good woman just helping to nurse and care for our guys and he took her from her room and he and his brothers raped her and cut her throat. I just didn't have enough evidence to prove anything more than he had been romancing her so he could steal medical supplies and sell 'em. Our guys needed those, and he used her to get access to the supplies. When she found out, he killed her."

"I know Jed, I know. Bad seed is all those boys are and I think the ones they ride with now are just as bad."

Jed sighed and stretched and said, "Well, we got

to move ahead. Think I will turn in. See you in the morning and we'll see about getting into Dallas and some work. Maybe hit up one of the ranches around here for puncher's wages."

"Texas and Pacific Rail Road just laid track into Dallas. Maybe there is work to be had there. Anyway, coffee at first light, and Jed, Jeff's a good boy he didn't mean no harm with that question 'bout the war and fight'n. He's been with me for two years now, ever since Ruth and I found him begging for food in Dallas. He's a hard worker and I have never had a problem with him."

"It's all fine my friend, I know he was just excited. War is always a romance for them that haven't been in it but it's a soul-killing, bitter business, war is. I hope he never has to drink from that cup."

Slapping his friend on the shoulder Craig said, "Turn in Jed, see you in the morning."

"Good night, my friend." And with that, Jed moved quietly off the porch and through the night to the barn.

Hours later, lying in the dark, with her man next to her, Ruth listened to Craig's ragged breathing, listened to his moans, felt his body tensing and thrash about in his sleep, gripped by the night terrors, by the memories of war and men dying. Was it every night the same dream or different each time? She didn't know, Craig never spoke of it in detail. She wondered if Jed Chance had the same dreams, the same horrible memories. He must have, she thought, he was with Craig all the way and besides, he was just a man.

Chapter 3

In the morning, after coffee, fry bread and the last remnants of the rabbits were eaten, Jed and Craig hooked up an old wagon and hit the trail for Dallas, and hopefully a job or two.

After an hour of traveling, Jed asked, "How long till we hit Dallas?"

"Oh, little after noon, I reckon."

"Well," Jed said as he started tugging at his old worn boot, "I got this." He turned up his boot and out dropped a $10-dollar gold piece. "Comanche didn't get everything."

"Damn, son! Ain't you just full of surprises!" smiled Craig.

"Yea, I figure it will get us some food, some cartridges for your Sharps and we'll see what else, but it won't fix that pump, though."

"No, surely not," said Craig.

"Ok, Craig, tell me how you met up with Ruth.

She seems like a fine woman, too fine to be running with the likes of you, I'm thinking."

"Hey, now, not so hard on your partner 'cause I got feelings!"

"Just blab it Pard."

"I met her in Dallas 'bout three years ago. She was a married school teacher in Alabama 'fore the war. When the war started her husband joined up with the Alabama Brigade and she helped with nursing the boys coming home. Her man was killed at Chickamauga. Toward the end of the war, she moved west to Texas, settled in Dallas, took to whoring a little just to get food to eat but never really full time at it."

"She gets no judgment from me, Craig. My mom was a whore. Let those that have never been starving and had no roof over their head do that. We all do what we have to and women—well, women have a tough row to hoe out here, especially if they are alone."

"I 'preciate that, Jed. She is a good woman and has been a good partner since we hooked up. When I met her, she was working on Camp Street at Doc Chamberlain's place. Probably one of the nicest of the drinking places on Camp Street. Least ways, nobody been killed there—yet."

"Heard of it, Camp Street I mean. I heard it was a tough place."

"Yep, it is. One end is a freedman's area and that's a place you don't want to find yourself in and the other end, the west end, is all saloons and places to gamble. Yea, getting down Camp Street is easy, getting out with your skin still on the bone, not so much."

"Well, let us not find ourselves on Camp Street. We got to be about our business."

"You're so right, Jed, so right. Anyways, we spoke 'bout getting hitched up and, well, maybe a kid or two but, just hadn't got 'round to it as yet. She's a good woman Jed. I love her and want to be with her."

"Understand my friend, I understand."

The wagon continued to wobble, creak and groan its way toward Dallas; the old horse, his head hanging and moving slowly toward the city and the friends dozing and talking and catching up on the years apart since the war.

It's nearly noon, it's hot, and dusty, Dallas in sight but now passing through a freedman's town, lying on the outskirts of the city, freed slaves, nowhere to go, no jobs, no money, and no hope, a desperate people living on the edge in so many ways.

In 1873, Dallas was a growing town of about three thousand souls and shaking off the effects of reconstruction, as was the entire state of Texas. It was growing, but could be a dangerous place.

"No iron," said Jed.

"What's that?"

"You're not carrying, Craig, and me, only this old colt. Makes me feel naked and you, well, you look strange not carrying. I never seen you without iron on your hip or in your hands."

"I know, it feels strange to me, too. I Left the Sharps with Ruth, not that it's much protection with just a few rounds and in such poor shape."

"Yea, well, we got to get back on our feet, all of us, you, me, Ruth and the boy and get that ranch going. We got to get right, right as rain."

Chapter 4

On the ride into Dallas, Jed and Craig had decided to seek employment at the Texas and Pacific. The T&P was putting in spurs on the northwest side of town in the direction of Fort Worth and since neither of the men had the kit necessary to start punching cows they agreed that working for the railroad would bring quicker work and quicker pay.

Jed and Craig had made it to the T&P office and were directed to the freight depot. There they met with Dave Turner, the hiring foreman. Turner had taken one look at Jed and figured the big man would have no problem carrying ties and rails, swinging a heavy hammer or unloading and loading freight and since they were a package deal and Craig looked fit and strong, he put both on the payroll. It was Friday afternoon and it was decided that they would start work on Monday. That would give the men time to get back to the ranch with whatever Jed's $10 would buy in the way of supplies and be back for work Monday morning.

As they were about to part ways until Monday, Turner looked at the two men and knowing they were busted and being a veteran of the war, albeit, for the blue, he decided to offer some help.

"We're done here boys but why don't you two come on down to Doc's place and let me buy you a drink and a bite? Later, you can come back here to the yard and sleep in one of the cars. I'll make it all right with the watchman 'fore we leave. I am going to front you each two dollars advance on account that you both smell like dead skunk. Head on over to Ma Belcher's across the yard there, get cleaned up and meet me back here in a couple of hours. Then we'll head over to Doc's just across the yard there on Camp Street."

As two friends headed toward the hot bath it was not lost on them that had said they would avoid Camp Street. They just smiled and shook their heads. They discussed the fact that while the railroad job would be better paying than the few dollars they would make in a month punching cows, it would still be a long while before they could get a ranch going and making money. After the much-needed cleanup, they headed back to meet Dave. They had enough money to get their clothes washed, but they weren't dry yet, so it was a bit uncomfortable walking back to the rail yard and both men pulled at their shirts and pants, fighting the ongoing chaffing.

Jed looked at Craig and said with a smile as he pulled on the seat of his wet pants, "Well, Pard, looks like we are going to Camp Street, despite our best intentions."

"Yea," said Craig. "But just for a bite to eat. Then we'll head on out of there."

They met up with Dave and headed to Doc's when suddenly gunshots rang out! Two, three in rapid succession, then followed by more, heavier firing. The gunfire seemed to be coming from around the corner. The three men, all former soldiers and use to the sounds of conflict, headed up the street and turned the corner, headed in the direction of the firing.

A driverless wagon tore past them, its terrified horses screaming, accompanied by more shots and the screaming of women and men yelling. Craig and Dave moved across the street and advanced at a crouch while Jed moved rapidly up his side. He came upon a woman lying in the street, the back of her head shot away, further up a man against a hitching post, his chest bloody and his lower jaw missing. Lying next to him was a Henry rifle. Jed scooped it up and tossed Craig his .36 Colt. Shots were still coming from around the corner. They found a wounded man huddled in a doorway, shot through the leg. "Robbers, they're robbing the bank, a passel of 'em!" the wounded man said.

"Dave, stay here with this gent; see if you can stop that leg from leaking! Come on Craig, let's take a look." Jed and Craig were moving toward the shooting before Dave could respond.

Jed and Craig turned the corner and saw six masked men on horseback sending lead up and down the street at anything moving. The street was full of dust and bucking and stamping horses. The yelling of men and screaming of women assailed their ears.

In front of them, four men crouched behind a wagon trying to return fire, one with a badge pinned to his chest. He saw Jed and Craig coming around the corner and he turned and aiming his pistol at them and asked, "Friend or foe?"

In answer, Jed quickly shouldered his found rifle and with two quick shots sent two of the desperadoes into the dust of the city's street.

Craig got off a shot, missed, fired again and saw

his target jerk and grab his shoulder, blood spurting through the man's fingers.

Both men knew immediately who the robbers were.

Suddenly, four masked figures emerged from the bank. Two were firing their pistols while two were each holding a struggling young woman, one blonde and one raven-haired, in front of them.

"Hold your fire! Hold it! Don't shoot no more!" yelled the Sheriff.

"That's right lawman! Everybody just stops slinging that lead or we kill these two sweet girls and leave them in the street!" shouted the big man with a yellow kerchief over his face and holding the struggling dark-haired girl.

All shooting stopped while the outlaws got to their horses and mounted up.

"All right," yelled the man with the yellow kerchief, "now we are leaving your fair town and taking the girls with us! Anybody follow us, these beauties die first! Tomorrow morning, first light, we don't see nobody on our trail, we'll put these little lovelies on a horse and send them back to ya! We want to thank you for your hospitality, Dallas! Maybe we'll visit you again sometimes!" Then hooting and hollering and firing their weapons at anything still moving, and with the two young girls screaming in desperation, the outlaws raced out of Dallas.

Chapter 5

The street was now a mass of yelling men, screaming women and terrified horses. The man with the badge was yelling out orders to men to check the bank for injured or killed and report back to him.

"Tom!" the man in charge yelled to a cowboy, "Get over to the telegraph office pronto and get a message to Fort Worth 'bout what happened here and tell 'em we need help in catching that scum that ran off with those girls! Tell 'em the Kerr and Gruber Bank has been robbed and girls stolen! Then gather up as many armed men as you can and meet me at my office in ten minutes ready to ride!"

A man came running from the bank holding a bloody rag to his head and with his shirt collar red with blood, "Sheriff, they took the Davidson girls, Rose, and Katherine! It was the Davidson girls, and 'bout eight thousand dollars cash!"

"Davidson's, you say?" responded the shocked

sheriff.

"Yes sir, they were in the bank with their grand-ma and her foreman. They beat him something awful, laughing the whole time and when the shooting started the one with the yella 'kerchief slapped Mrs. Davidson to the floor and he and one with him grabbed the girls up!"

"Goddammit," uttered the sheriff, "Just damn it to hell!" Then, "Jess, go get the doc and get him over there to check on Mrs. Davidson and her man. We got people in the street needs help, too."

Jed and Craig had been watching the unfolding of events and listening. Jed spoke up, "You the sheriff, I would guess."

In the excitement, the sheriff had forgotten about the two strangers who had appeared from nowhere and now he turned and took in the two men.

"Sheriff Barkley, James Barkley and who might you be?"

"My name is Jed Chance, and this is my pard, Craig Mullins."

"Know of you Mullins, you and your woman ranching to the west, over the other side of the Trinity a piece."

"Yep, that'll be us and a boy named, Jeff."

"Well, appreciate you two jump'n in when you did." Turning to Jed, he said, "You did for two, and your partner there dusted one, too, or, at least, got a piece of 'em."

"Glad we could help out," said Jed. "And Sheriff, there won't be no telegraph line operating, and if you are going after those men, take a lot of men with you and pick single men."

Taken aback by Jed's comment, Barkley asked, "Now, why would I do that?"

"Fewer widows," said Craig.

Sheriff Barkley stood for a moment, staring at these two men, and then asked, "How do you know they'll be no telegraph?"

Jed and Craig looked at each other, unspoken knowledge passing between them.

Jed said, "'Cause those boys are former rebel raiders. They rode behind the northern lines raiding towns and causing hell for three years for those folks in the north. The first thing they would 'a done 'fore riding in here was to cut the line, probably three or four places."

"And how would you know all this?"

In measured tones, Jed replied, "'Cause we once rode with 'em. I led 'em, least ways a few of 'em. You got three brothers, Sam, Bob and Randy Rogers. Sam, he'll be the leader, the one with the yellow kerchief, and a mean man. All three of those boys are mean and those riding with 'em is mean sons of bitches. Men, women, children, makes no difference with those hombres. I wouldn't look for 'em to turn those girls back to 'ya either."

At that moment, two tough and capable-looking cowboys ran up to the sheriff, each loaded for bear.

"We got twelve, thirteen men ready to go and one's bringing up your horse." One of the men said to the Sheriff while looking suspiciously at Jed and Craig.

"Bev, this here is, — excuse me, what did you say your name was?"

"Jed, Jed Chance."

The man called Bev nodded and after a moment of staring at Jed, said, "Chance? There was a Jed Chance sheriff'n down in south Texas 'round Medallion and other places and got his self quite a rep. He's supposed to be really handy with a gun, really fast, big fella too. You him?"

"Suppose so. Don't think there would be two of

us."

Craig looked at his friend and started to speak but—

Barkley spoke up, "Chance, Mullins, these two are Bev and Tom Scott, my two deputies."

The men nodded at each other.

"Bev, watch the town. Try to get everyone calmed down and make sure you check on Mrs. Davidson. Let her know we are headed out and we'll bring those two girls back to her mighty fast."

The posse arrived in a cloud of dust and snorting animals and with the Sheriff's horse.

"You boys are more than welcome to come along. We probably could use 'ya," said Barkley, as he mounted up.

"No guns and no horses," said Craig, "but our best to you boys, good luck!"

"And sheriff," said Jed, "ya'll be watchful for an ambush. They'll want to catch you unawares and whittle your posse down."

Sheriff Barkley stared at Jed for a moment then waved at the two friends as he and the posse left the town of Dallas at speed and with determination to bring back the young girls.

Chapter 6

Over the weekend, Craig and Jed returned to the ranch with flour, bacon, coffee and potatoes given to them by grateful townspeople after Bev Scott had related to many of them what the two had done to help drive off the outlaws. Ruth and Jeff were glad to see them and the provisions. Jeff couldn't get enough of hearing about the robbery and the gun fight. Both Jed and Craig thought they would talk themselves hoarse with the repeated telling of the story. The only part they left out was of Jed killing two of the outlaws. It wasn't something Jed wanted Jeff to know about just yet.

On Monday morning bright and early, Jed and Craig presented themselves at the railroad warehouse and after some directions given by Dave Turner, they began work loading up rail cars with buffalo hides destined for market in Chicago and New York.

Along about lunchtime, Dave entered the rail car where they were stacking hides and said to Jed and

Craig, "Sheriff is back. He came into town a few minutes ago with the posse, lest ways what's left of it." He dropped his head, "Looks like about four died and several more were wounded."

Jed asked, "And the girls?"

"No, they aren't with them."

"Shit," said Craig. "I knew things were going to go bad for those boys, just knew it."

"Well, they should have the telegraph lines back up by now and word will go out to Fort Worth. The blue coats will get out after the Rogers boys and their crew, if they haven't already," said Jed.

Jed and Craig went back to work and Dave wondered off to his office.

An hour or so later, while sitting in the door of the rail car taking a break, Jed poked the dozing Craig in the ribs.

"What! What 'cha do that for? I was just taking Ruthie in my arms and—,"

"Well, finish that though later, we got company." Coming across the yard was Dave Turner, Sheriff Barkley, his deputy Bev, another man, and a short, slightly rotund silvered -haired lady of some age dressed in fancy black finery but with a determined, no-nonsense air about her. The group approached the two friends.

Barkley, looking tired, worried and with a bandage showing from under his right shirt sleeve, said, "Jed, Craig, this here is Mrs. Davidson, wife of the late Emanuel Davidson and owner of one of the biggest horse and cattle ranches in Texas. It was Mrs. Davidson's granddaughters, Rose, and Katherine that were taken by the Rogers gang. 'Course you both know about that. Anyways, she wants to speak with you and —."

Mrs. Davidson, interrupting the Sheriff said, "I got no time for long-winded talk, sheriff. Now, you two are Mr. Chance and Mr. Mullins, is that right?

"Yes, that'd be right, Mrs. Davidson," said Jed.

"Well, fine. My girls are gone. Rose, she's twenty-three and Katherine is twenty. They are good, wonderful girls, both taken by those outlaws and my foreman is dead, beaten to death by those vicious animals! I want my girls back and back damn quick! Now, the sheriff tells me about what you two did to help during the robbery and Bev says that you, Mr. Chance, were once a lawman and a good one. More importantly, you two seem to know these outlaws. So, I want to hire you two to go after these sons of the devil and rescue my girls and return them to me. I'll pay and pay well."

"Mrs. Davidson, we certainly respect your feeling and grieve mightily about the loss of your young ladies and your foreman, but we just ain't equipped to chase no outlaws, particularly this here group of bad men. Craig and I both are going through some tough times and trying to get a horse ranch started and—"

"I know what you are doing! I know about that hardscrabble ranch over by the Trinity and your plans. Mr. Turner here has related all of that to me. How long is it going to take you working like this to raise enough money to get a horse ranch up and running? Five, ten years if you are lucky, and here I am offering good money. It's a chance to get what you need right now."

"Mrs. Davidson, we got no noise makers, no horses, and no kit. None of the things we would need to go off chasing this bunch. 'Sides, I would guess the Calvary over at Fort Worth would be headed out after those outlaws or the sheriff here can head back out," said Craig.

"Cavalry can't right now. Some Kiowa bucks run off from the reservation and are stirring up a mess. Those soldier boys are trying to get those injuns corralled up," said Barkley, "and Belle Starr and her bunch are rustling cattle and stealing horses from Mrs. Henderson and other ranches in the area, so I got my hands full there. 'Sides, ain't got any posse volunteers after what happened to the last bunch."

Stepping away from the others, Mrs. Davidson motioned for Jed and Craig to follow her. Jed looked at Sheriff Barkley who just shrugged and motioned for them to go with her.

After moving off some distance from the group, she turned and spoke quietly but firmly to Jed and Craig, "Now you listen here you two. We must move and move fast to save my girls. I will pay you each two thousand dollars when you bring back the girls. Plus, I will give you a starter herd of thirty broodmares and three stallions to start your ranch and I will outfit you, lock, stock, and barrel with whatever you need to have to bring back my young ones." Tears glistened in the old lady's eyes, but her look remained determined as she finished speaking.

Jed and Craig were stunned and momentarily speechless. They stood, looking first at Mrs. Davidson then each other, then the ground, shuffling their old boots, both lost in thought.

After a few moments of silence, Craig spoke up, "I want one other thing."

"Wait, you sure Pard, that this—"

"Yep, I'm sure and if you stop and think about it, so are you, Jed. She's right. It will take years 'fore we can say we got us a horse ranch. With what she's offering, it will be some mite sooner that we'll have that ranch up and running."

"Might be they'll be bury'n us on that ranch."

"What other thing do you want, Mr. Mullins?" asked Mrs. Davidson.

"I need a water pump. My water pump at the ranch is busted to hell. I would want that fixed so I ain't so worried 'bout Ruth and the boy having to haul water from the Trinity."

"Done!" the woman exclaimed, "that, and I'll send a month of food and supplies to 'em to boot. I know your...I know Ruth. I'll go see her and I will make it right with her. I know it won't be easy, but she's a westerner. She'll, see the right of it. Do we have a deal?"

The two old friends stood looking at each other. Each weighing the reward and risks, and possible cost of going after the Rogers gang. Jed looked off in the distance, kicked the dust off ruined boots, then turning to the desperate woman said, "OK, Mrs. Davidson, we got a deal. We'll go fetch your girls back, but you must know—"

"Mr. Chance, I know the risk. I know that there is a good chance my old eyes will never lay sight on my babies again, but I have to try Mr. Chance, I have to try."

The woman's trembling voice and her shaking hand that grasped his own hand with such strength and determination and the look in the old woman's eyes convinced Jed that he and Craig had chosen the right path.

"OK, Mrs. Davidson, we'll get the gear fetched up if you will tell us where to go and who to see," said Jed.

"Luke! Luke get over here!" called out Mrs. Davidson.

"Yes, yes, Mrs. Davison?" responded her new foreman, as he quickly walked to where Davison, Chance and Mullins were standing.

"Take Mr. Chance and Mr. Mullins over to Alexander Sanger's store and get them fitted out stem to stern, top to bottom. Whatever they need, they get. Tell Alexander to put it all on my bill. Turning to Jed and Craig, "This is Luke Davis, my new foreman."

The three men shook hands.

"Luke, after they get their gear, get 'em over to

the gunsmith and get' em heeled. Then take them down to the stockyard where we have those horses we are shipping to Fort Concho and get 'em some horses from that group. Good ones. They can pick what they want."

Turning to Craig, she said, "If things don't go well, you know, you don't make it back, don't worry 'bout Ruth and the boy. I'll make sure they don't go wanting. Mr. Chance, do you have —"

"No." He cut her off, "Got only myself to see to, 'cepting my friend here and his family."

"OK, Mr. Chance. When do you think you can head out?"

"No later than noon tomorrow, I should think."

"OK, I'll meet you at the sheriff's office at nine in the morning. I should think that is close enough to noon to get started."

With that, Mrs. Henderson turned and accompanied by Dave Turner, the sheriff and his deputy left the three men standing in the rail yard.

As Jed and Craig watched the feisty little lady leave, Jed asked, "So, my friend, what are you gon'a do 'bout telling Ruth and Jeff 'bout your plans to go chase these outlaws?"

"Well, I hadn't rightly thought on it 'fore you

said something," Craig said, as he turned to Jed. "I got no time to get to the ranch and back with all we got to do, so I guess, well, I guess I'll just write a note and let her know. Mrs. Henderson says she'll talk to her, but Lord knows she ain't gon'a be happy, but I do figure this is best for us. I do think that."

"Well, I hope you're right, Craig, and I hope you can write a good letter to Ruth or those Rogers boys and their crew might be easier than a facing off with your woman all agitated at 'ya."

"Damned if that ain't the truth of it, Jed. Well, we'll fetch those girls back and the next time I have to be face to face with Ruth, we'll have pockets full of money and a herd of horses. That'll smooth things over."

"Umm, well, maybe you aren't all smart 'bout women as I once thought. Anyhow, we got a lot to do, so let's get a move on."

Chapter 7

At Jed's insistence, they headed over to the gun-smith first. Once there, Jed and Craig looked over the side arms available, a variety of powder and ball revolvers by Remington, Navy Colts, a couple of Schofield revolvers and were about to pick out a couple of Colt 1860 revolvers when Luke spoke to the gunsmith.

"Mrs. Davidson has hired these two boys to fetch back her girls. Make sure they get the best you got there, Henry, Mrs. Davidson's foot'n the bill."

"Well," drawled Henry, "then, step over to this here case and take a look at this new wheel gun from Colt. I think that they call it their Colt .45 strap gun, or pistol, or some such. Army has done bought a bunch for the troops. It's what them boys is using now. These are actual meant for the fort but seeings as how it's the Henderson girls and all...well, I guess these got lost in the shipment or some such."

Jed and Craig strode over to the glass- topped

display case while Henry pulled out a couple of the new Colts from a wooden case and laid them on the counter.

"It's .45 caliber center-fire with a 40-grain cartridge shoving a 255-gram lead bullet down the barrel. A fine weapon it is for sure," said Henry.

"Why's it called, 'back strap?" asked Craig as he reached for one of the guns.

"It's the strong strap of metal running from the butt to over the cylinder, gives the gun strength."

Jed and Craig each picked one of the new revolvers and began testing the action, the spin of the cylinder, sighting down the barrel and testing the heft and feel of the weapon.

"Yea, yea, I like it, like it a lot," said Jed. "I'll be needing two of these here."

"Yep, give me a couple of 'em too," said Craig.

"Sure thing, boys, but a little warning for 'ya when you load them lead throwers up, drop the hammer on an empty chamber. Heard tell some of those Calvary boys been accidently shot when the hammer was on a live round and the revolver got jostled or such".

Setting their new six-shooters aside, the two friends turned to the rifle rack. They were looking at the 44-40 Yellow Boys when the gunsmith spoke up.

"Luke here says Mrs. Davidson wants you two to have the best so step back here for a minute." He led the men to a storeroom in the back where several crates were being unpacked. Reaching under the straw of one of the crates he pulled out a new lever action rifle.

"This is the new Winchester 73 model in 44-40. What do you think?" he said as he handed the rifle to Jed. Jed worked the action and sighted down the barrel, bringing the rifle quickly up to his shoulder several times.

"You got this with a shorter barrel?"

"Yep, I got a carbine, right here and a nice one too," the gunsmith said as he handed Jed a shorter version of the rifle that he took from another crate.

"I'll take this," said Jed, hefting the Winchester. "And two of the Colts and that William Moore coach gun in the rack behind the counter."

As the group began moving back into the main shop area Craig said, "I am good with this here Winchester, two of those strap guns and I'll take a coach gun too. We'll need 50 rounds each for the scatter guns, 100 rounds each for the rifles and same for the pistols. Oh, and we'll each take one of them bowie knives in the cabinet over yonder."

"Damn, you two going after an army?" asked Henry as he began gathering the requested items and placing them on the counter top.

"Yahoos we're after take a lot of killing," replied Craig.

Jed picked up one of his new side arms, dropped in five rounds and let the hammer down on an empty chamber and stuck the gun in his waistband. He did the same with the other pistol.

Craig had been looking at holsters, the Slim Jim and Mexican Loop and picked out two of the Loop holsters and belts. He tossed one to Jed and belted his around his waist and holstering one of his now loaded pistols he looked at Jed and smiled, "Damn, damn son, if this don't feel right!"

"You look right too, Pard."

Turning to Luke, Jed asked, "Where's the saddle maker?"

"Over on the west side of the town square, name of Padgitt, Clint, and Jesse Padgitt."

"Let's head over there next. They got some work to do," said Jed.

Turning to the gunsmith Jed said, "OK, now hand me down two of those holsters there, no belts, just the holsters."

Handing Jed two holsters the gunsmith asked, "What's with the two holsters and no belt?

"I'm gon'a get the saddle maker to sew them on cross draw like on our gun belts. If'n you be on a running horse it just be easier to pull cross draw than trying to fetch iron off'n the side, leastways, I like it better."

"Henry, get that ammo and stuff delivered over to the hotel for us and leave the bill there so I can get it to Mrs. Davidson," said Luke.

"Will do, Luke, and tell Mrs. Davidson the ammo is on me. Hope them girls come back safe and sound, surely do."

"Thanks, Henry, I'll let her know."

And with that, the trio headed out.

"Padgitt saddles, I heard of 'em," said Jed.

"Yep, they make that Bronco Brand saddle that's popular with the boys. They got a brother, Tom. He's got a place down in Waco. Good men, the Padgitt boys," said Luke.

Arriving at the saddle shop the men quickly picked out two dark leather saddles with scabbards for their long guns.

Then Jed said to Jesse Padgitt, "Need you to fix

on these saddles, right behind the horn, a loop for our coach guns and how 'bout sewing these here holsters on our belts, so we can get at 'em cross draw."

"I can do that," replied Padgitt.

"And I need you to do some work on this here holster," said Jed, as he took his holster rig off his shoulder and handed it to Jesse Padgitt.

"Looks new, looks in excellent shape. What do you need to be done to it?" asked Padgitt.

"Cut it down. I want you to cut the end off, 'bout two inches and cut down the top of the holster an inch or so. I want to have the gun come out fast and clean without rubbing on much. Then sew on a strong strap that will go over the hammer so it don't fall out when I'm riding. Craig, you want 'em to cut yours down too?"

Craig, who had been looking at Jed with a confused expression replied, "No, I mean — no. I never have seen that done. Where'd you get that idea from?"

"Just an idea I came up with when I was working down south Texas."

"I'll just keep mine like it is. It's fine with me," said Craig.

"Suit yourself, Pard."

"Oh, and we need this by morning, 'bout eight,"

said Jed.

Mr. Padgitt's brow furrowed, "Look here, it's already getting on in the afternoon and—"

"Mr. Padgitt," said Luke, "these here fellows are going out after Mrs. Henderson's girls and they got to get started as soon as possible. She's foot'n all the bills, for everything. If you could—"

"Well, should 'a told me up front! Everything will be ready by eight, even if we have to work all night. And please, tell Mrs. Henderson there will only be funds due for the saddles. No charge for the extra things wanted."

"Thanks so much, Mr. Padgitt," said Luke.

After grabbing up bridles and horse blankets, the three men left the saddle maker and went to the blacksmith's shop where Jed and Craig had the front sights filed off their pistols then went to the stockyard to pick out horses.

Craig picked out a buckskin horse with a blaze face and Jed a big, dark chestnut mare with white mane and tail.

"You always did like flashy horse flesh," said Craig as the men put bridles on their horses.

"Yep, can't help myself when it comes to pretty

horses."

"Hey, Luke, snake out a strong one for pack horse duty," called out Jed.

"Will do, Jed, tie your mounts up to the rail and head over to Sanger's store. I'll see to the horses getting boarded and fed at the stable and catch up with you there."

At Sanger's, Jed and Craig picked out new boots, long johns, pants, blue wool shield front shirts, new hats with stampede strings and shotgun chaps. They stocked up on coffee, beans, bacon, can goods, some cooking gear, tobacco, and other essentials and asked that they be delivered to the hotel. The store was closing when Luke showed up and gave Mr. Sanger the instructions to send the bill for everything to Mrs. Henderson.

Turning to Jed and Craig, Mr. Sanger said, "Words around on what you two gents are going to try and do. We wish you Godspeed and bring our girls home! Luke, you tell Mrs. Henderson I am only going to bill her for the clothes. The food and other supplies are my gifts."

"Thank you ever so much Mr. Sanger. I will surely let Mrs. Henderson know."

Walking to the hotel, the men were silent, each

lost in his own thoughts. As they arrived at the front of the hotel, Luke turned to the two friends.

"Jed, Craig, we love those girls. Since Mr. Henderson died and the girls' momma and dad were killed by Kiowa, they're 'bout all Mrs. Henderson has left for family and she is all they have. You got clothes, guns, horses, and food. Is there anything else, anything at all you need?"

Craig looked at Jed, and Jed looked hard into Luke's eyes and said, "Luck, a lot of luck."

Chapter 8

Just before eight o'clock Tuesday morning, Craig and Jed were just finishing up breakfast at the hotel and their conversation on the dangerous task they were undertaking, and the challenges they faced. As they started to rise, taking last gulps of coffee, Jessie Padgitt walked in carrying their pistol rigs. He was smiling as he tossed them to Jed and Craig.

"Here you go, boys. Give 'em a try."

Jed belted on his new holsters and removing his guns from his waistband, he slid one into his cross-draw holster on the left side and secured it and then slid the other into his new, cut-down holster. With the sight filed off and not much leather holding the noise maker, it slid in smooth and easy.

Craig admired the new holsters and said to Jed, "Let's see you —"

A blur, a flash! Later, at lunch with Sheriff Barkley, Jessie Padgitt would say it was the fastest thing he had ever seen. One moment the gun was in its holster and then, faster than thought, it was out.

Craig stared, eyes wide, taken aback at what he had just witnessed. In the war, Jed was always fast afoot and with his hands or a knife, but their side arms were always in a flap holster. He had never seen such from Jed.

As Jed returned the pistol to its resting place and secured it, Craig said, "Damn, friend! I never have seen you — I mean when, uh, when — "

"Places I been, places I traveled to. Lots of time on my hands so, well, I practiced. I've always had a way with guns, and knives. They always fit my hand and, well, I am what I am. A man that is just good with guns."

Craig started to speak again but at that moment Luke stepped into the dining area and said, "Craig, I got your horse here and the pack horse. Let's get you boys loaded up."

"Craig's horse? "How 'bouts mine, you expecting me to be walking to fetch those girls?" asked Jed.

"Well, no Jed, but Mrs. Henderson nixed the horse you had picked out and sent a couple of the boys out last night to fetch a horse from the ranch. They should be showing up any time now and I think you'll like it."

Mr. Padgitt departed with words of encouragement and good luck to all and Craig and Jed moved their supplies to the porch of the hotel and began loading their pack horse. Jed was just finishing the last tightening of straps and Craig was adjusting his stirrups when Sheriff Barkley appeared.

"Sheriff, you never told us what happened when you went after the gang. How did they surprise you?" asked Craig.

"Well, we were between here and Plano. We had cut their sign right away and they were easy to follow. Mostly flat ground between here and Plano so didn't think much about an ambush. Then, well...then we were crossing a creek and they just rose up, out of nowhere. One minute the creek-bed was open, and then they just come out of the ground. They had buried themselves. I guess four of them, and once they commenced to firing, the others came charging down on us from upstream. Shot us to pieces. I should've listened to you boys."

"How's that?" asked Jed.

"I should've left the married men in town."

A commotion caused the men to turn and they saw Mrs. Henderson, followed by a few of her cowboys and some of the townspeople approaching. One of her ranch hands was leading a big, coal-black horse with the longest, thickest flowing mane and tail Jed had ever seen. With furred hoofs and powerful shoulders, legs long and lean and a long, arched neck, it was a spectacular looking animal. Not a speck of any other color but black could be found on the prancing mare. It wore Jed's saddle. Neither man had ever seen a horse like this one.

"What the hell is that?" asked Craig.

"Don't know pard but it's a muscled-up son-of-a—" started Jed but then stopped himself due to the presence of Mrs. Henderson.

Mrs. Henderson took the reins from her ranch hand and led the horse over to Jed and put them in his big hands.

"It's a Friesian, Mr. Chance. A horse prized by the knights of Europe. They needed a horse strong enough to carry them when wearing their armor into battle but still nimble and quick of foot. They once were found in the northeastern states, but they seemed to die out. I had six mares and a stallion brought over from Germany to try and re-introduce the breed as a drafting horse. Anyway, you're a big man Jed and you need a powerful horse. She's yours. You name her, I never did."

Jed stroked the horse's neck and let his hands hold her cheeks as her muzzle buried in his chest and the mare breathed his scent in. Then he ran his hands over her withers, shoulders and forearms, letting her get use to his touch, then her buttocks and hind quarters. The entire time he talked softly to her, getting her used to his voice.

"She's a beauty, Mrs. Henderson. I'll put her to good use."

Jed began loading his new horse with supplies and his coach gun and rifle.

"Well, you two look like you could fight off a whole passel of bad men. You ready to go?" asked Mrs. Henderson.

Craig turned to Luke and handed him a bundle. "That's some powder and shot and Jed's old pistol. Most appreciative if you could get that to my Ruth and the boy when you take those supplies out to 'em. I got a letter here for Ruth. She don't know what we got going on so, well, she's gon'a be pissed. Luke, tell 'em I love 'em and should be back in a couple of weeks or so".

"Will do, Craig and I got an old shotgun and shells I will drop with this also."

"Thanks, Luke. Much obliged."

Then turning to Mrs. Henderson, Craig said, "Yes, Ma'am, we are ready." With that Craig mounted his horse and took up the lead to the pack horse.

Jed started to mount but Mrs. Henderson reached out, put her hand on his arm and stopped him. He turned and looked down into the old woman's eyes. She spoke to him softly.

"Jed, may I call you Jed?"

"Yes Ma'am, you can."

"Good, that's good. Now, the Sheriff tells me that, according to you, these are mean, mean men."

"Yes ma'am, that's the truth of it."

Her hand reached up and gently traced the scar that ran down the right side of his face. As she traced the jagged line she asked, "How did this happen?"

"Was a man with a knife."

"Did you kill him?"

"Yes, Ma'am, I did."

Taking her hand from his face and holding one of his big hands with her two she asked, "And you Jed, are you a mean man?"

Jed looked away, looked far off in the distance and remembered moments from his past and remembering those things he looked at the lady and said, "Yes, yes, I am a mean man. I can be just as mean as those outlaws."

With a firm conviction in her voice, she whispered, "Good! That's good, Jed! If you find my girls dead or — or spoiled, you kill those sons-of-bitches that did it! Kill 'em and leave their bodies to rot and their bones to bleach in the sun!" And then in a soft whisper and a tear sliding down her cheek, she asked, "Can you do that for me, Jed, for me and my girls, can you promise me that?"

Jed looked down at this tearful woman and remembered the war and a young girl brutalized and killed by these very same men and said, "Yes, I will. I promise. I will do this for you and yours."

"Thank you, Jed, thank you for that. Now, go with God."

With that, Jed mounted his horse, looked, for a moment at the hopeful faces staring back at him and with a look and a nod of his head at Craig they spurred their horses north toward Plano.

Jed knew, and had known, since the afternoon of the robbery that there was no hope for those young girls. And since there was no hope for the girls and with the promise he had just made, there was no hope for those that took them.

Chapter 9

It was early Wednesday morning on the Mullins ranch and Ruth was busy sweeping the porch of the house when Jeff, walking over from the barn, called out, "Ruth, check out that cloud of dust to the east. Looks like we're gon'a have some visitors from Dallas, a passel of 'em by the looks of it."

Ruth shaded her eyes as she looked where Jeff was pointing. She could just make out horses and what appeared to be wagons headed toward the Ranch.

"Might be its Craig and Jed but I don't know what they would be coming home for nor who they would be bringing with 'em." Then she offered a prayer, "Lord, don't let anything have happened to my man or Jed."

They stood together and watched and soon they could make out eight or ten riders and three wagons loaded down with lumber and other supplies. Ruth could see Mrs. Henderson sitting in the first wagon and immediately her heart went out to the lady as she thought about the recent robbery and the taking of the Henderson girls. Her mind was full of thoughts on the unfortunate girls but also wondering why these people were riding into her ranch yard.

The wagon carrying Mrs. Henderson pulled up to the porch while the riders began to dismount and tie up at various hitching spots around the ranch yard.

"Hello, Mrs. Henderson. It is so good to see you," said Ruth, as she approached the wagon where Mrs. Henderson's foreman, Luke, was helping her down.

"Hello Ruth, it's good to see you and the boy. Jeff, isn't it? Yes, I remember, Jeff. Craig talked mighty nice on you, Jeff. He says you're a good boy." Said Mrs. Henderson as she gently ran her hand over Jeff's hair.

"Thanks, ma'am, uh, Mrs. Henderson, that's mighty kind of 'ya," said Jeff.

"Mrs. Henderson, Craig told us about what happened to Rose and Katherine. I am so very sorry, and I hope they get brought back home soon," said Ruth.

"Thanks Ruth. I'm in a constant state of prayer on it. It's about my girls and Mr. Mullins and his friend, Jed, that causes me to be here."

"Craig and Jed, what's going on? Are they alright? And the wagons, what's all this stuff for? What's going on?" asked Ruth.

"Well, hold on a minute and we'll get to that, and we have a letter for you from Craig." said Mrs. Henderson. Then turning to Luke, she said, "Luke, set a couple of boys to putting in that new water pump and set the others to getting to work on building the corrals. One for breaking broncs and the other to hold 'em. Ruth and I will get the supplies into the house."

Then, turning to an increasing confused and nervous Ruth, she said, "Help me get this food into the house, Ruth. We brought a passel of food for you and Jeff." Mrs. Henderson moved to the back of wagon and began to pick up several boxes.

"Mrs. Henderson, what is all this? What's going on?

Stopping for a moment, Mrs. Henderson looked at Ruth and said. "Ruth, help me get these things in the house and I will tell you all about it, I promise. Have you any drinking spirits in the house?"

"Why, yes, a little whiskey is all."

"Good, 'cause I think we're both going to need it. Now, grab hold of a box or two and let's get this done."

For a moment Ruth just stared at the old woman

hustling around the wagon, then just shaking her head she pitched in to move the food into the house.

An hour or so later, Ruth stood in the doorway to the little house. Her eyes were red from crying and she nervously twisted her apron in her hands as she watched the men in the yard, some building corrals and a few others finishing with putting in the new water pump.

From behind her, sitting in a chair at the table, Mrs. Henderson said, "I'm sorry Ruth. There just wasn't any other way that I could see. I am a desperate woman and your Craig and Jed Chance seemed to be my only hope. Please forgive me for bringing this worry into your life, but try to see it from my side of the fence, please."

Turning back into the house, Ruth walked toward Mrs. Henderson, "Oh, I see it Mrs. Henderson. If I was in your place and given all you had to go on then might be I would do the same thing."

"Mr. Mullin and Jed both rode with those outlaws. Surely, when they catch up to them they should be able to reason with 'em and win my girls back. To hell with the banks money, I'll replace that, but I need my girls back. And Ruth, that Jed, from what I hear he was a law man in south Texas and he sure sets his hat as a man that can get this kind of job done."

Ruth stopped in the middle of pouring herself a cup of coffee and turning to Mrs. Henderson she said, "If half the stories Craig told about Jed and what he did in the war are true then those men that took Rose and Katherine are in a pile of trouble, but Mrs. Henderson, it's about Craig. He's not who he was in the war. Craig... he...well, he's not a mean man, not a killing man, least ways not anymore. He has bad dreams almost every night about the killings in the war. Those dead men visit him, and he suffers for it. I don't know how he's gon'a react to things if they catch up to those outlaws."

"Well, he seemed fine when they left. Look, Ruth, Craig's first thought was for you and Jeff. I offered the money and horses so y'all could get this ranch started now and not have to wait for years to get it up and running." Mrs. Henderson rose from the table and taking Ruth by the shoulders she said, "It's all going to work out. It must. Certainly, the evil of those outlaws can't win out. Please, Ruth, stay positive with me, please."

Ruth laid her hand on Mrs. Henderson shoulder, "For the sake of your girls and you, Jeff and me, I will be praying on it and believing every day that all will be fine, but I will have fear in my belly every day until

Craig and Jed get home."

At that moment Jeff came running into the house shouting, "They got it working! The new water pump is working! No more hauling water from the Trinity!"

Ruth smiled at Jeff and said, "That is a relief! Now, get on over and help get those corrals built. We're gon'a have horses to fill them up and right soon."

"Yipee! Horses on the ranch! Man! Craig and Jed are gon'a be surprised!" Jeff turned and headed out the door.

Ruth and Mrs. Henderson watched him go.

"Are you going to tell him?"

"Yes, when the time is right, but not right now. Now, it's getting late and those hands of yours have probably worked up a frightful hunger. I need to get some food for 'em."

"No need. I got cookie to bring a mess of food for the boys. I'll get him to get started cooking it up. It's nothing for you to fret over, Ruth." With that Mrs. Henderson went out to the yard to get her cook busy with preparing food for all.

The work went late into the day, so it was decided that everyone would spend the night at the ranch. Ruth offered Mrs. Henderson the use of her bed, but the old woman wouldn't hear of it. She said she would be perfectly comfortable sleeping in the back of one of wagons, and so she did.

Later, all were sleeping, save one. Ruth laid awake staring into the darkness and thinking about Craig and fearing for his and Jed's safely. She also thought of something else. She didn't know how Craig would react when and if things came to gun play but she was afraid. She was afraid that if it did come to that and if Craig hesitated and it cost Jed his life, Craig would never recover. His body might survive but as a man, he would be lost forever. She shivered with the weight of it all, closed her eyes and cried.

The next morning, Mrs. Henderson's crew had breakfast and finished the corrals and left the ranch. Ruth and Mrs. Henderson gave each other a final hug before the old woman climbed up on her wagon.

"Try not to worry too much, child. Those two will find those girls and all of 'em will return home safe. I promise. I would not tolerate otherwise." said Mrs. Henderson, as she gazed down at Ruth.

"I'll trust the good Lord will look after 'em and bring them home safe. I'll be telling Jeff after you leave so wish me luck with that," said Ruth.

"You'll do fine, Ruth. I'll stay in touch and send a couple of boys over every few days to check on you two."

"Thank you that would be nice. Goodbye."

"Bye, Ruth." Then turning to her driver Mrs. Henderson said, "Put the leather to 'em Jeb and let's get on home."

Ruth stood in the yard watching the wagon and the riders as they moved back toward Dallas. Then she looked toward the new corrals and watched Jeff as he climbed on the freshly cut boards and was having a conversation with some imaginary foe as his pointed finger sent out a hail of imaginary bullets toward his pretend bad man. It was a fine morning. The sun was bright and a breeze moved the trees and across the yard and tugged at her hair. A raven landed on the corral, just a few yards from where Jeff played, and Ruth suddenly felt cold and fearful. A Raven in times of trouble was never a good sign. She bent and picked up a rock intending to throw it at the evil bird but before she could raise her arm it flew off. Ruth looked to the north, thinking that would be where Craig and Jed were. Somewhere out there they searched for bad men. She stared hard, trying to will Craig to appear, riding toward the safety of the ranch. With a big sigh she figured she should get the conversation with Jeff over with.

"Jeff, come on over to the porch. We need to talk on something. It's kind of important."

Jeff jumped off the top rail of the corral and ran to the porch.

"Boy, Ruth, ain't it something! It looks like a real ranch now! We..."

Seeing the look on Ruth's face caused Jeff to stop and stare at her.

"What is it, Ruth? What's going on?"

"Well, Jeff, it has to do with Craig and Mr. Chance...uh...Jed. They are up to something and you best be knowing."

And so, she told him.

Chapter 10

A hundred or so miles west and south of Plano, Texas, next to a flowing creek surrounded by trees of pecan, cottonwood, and oak, Sam Rogers and his two brothers, Randy, and Bob sat around a small fire drinking coffee. They had been in the encampment for almost three days partly due to a wounded man and partly to enjoy the female spoils of the robbery. In the trees behind them, several of their men were laughing and yelling as they finished their morning sport with Rose, the older of the two Henderson girls. They, all of them, had been at her off and on throughout the night, as they had been the night before. Sam had tried to keep the men off the girls for as longs as possible. It wasn't out of any care for the girls, but because he knew they may have to use them as bargaining chips if they were caught. After a day or so of holding the men off, he finally gave in. Of course, part of it was because he wanted some of that blonde, older girl too.

The younger of the two girls, Katherine, was tied up and lying next to the fire. She was dirty, her clothing torn, and her tear-streaked face was swollen and bruised from Sam Rogers repeatedly slapping her to get her to stop crying during the night. She was hungry and terrified but wanted to be strong for Rose. Katherine could not see what was happening to her sister, but she knew. The men had been with her older sister for most of two days. Katherine was sick at heart and in spirit and desperate to think of something, some way to help her sister. The sisters were quite a contrast. The older was Rose, a young lady of short stature and a voluptuous figure, flowing blonde hair and blue eyes and then Katherine, a tall, willowy ebony haired lady. They were both strong willed women that didn't frighten easily and were proud of their heritage of being decedents of some of the earliest settlers to the Dallas area. When the men came for Rose, both women fought against them with all the strength they could muster but when one of the men pulled a knife and held it to Katherine's throat and told Rose if she didn't go with them quietly he would cut the younger one's throat, the girls stopped fighting. Katherine yelled and screamed but Rose quieted her and told her everything would be ok. She assured

Katherine that their grandmother would not abandon them, and that help would come and come soon. Rose said she could handle what was to come. The girl didn't know how bad it was going to be.

"Need to get moving," said Sam. "Could be a posse or some blue coats on our trail and could be showing up anytime."

"Right, big brother, but we need to do something 'bout Jeff, though. That shoulder wound is getting worse. Maybe we find a doc somewhere," said Bob.

"No docs 'round here. Get them boys off'n that bitch and let's break camp. I'll check up on Jeff."

Motioning toward where the men were gathered, "You gon'a want a slice of that 'fore we get started?" asked his brother Bob.

"Naw, I ain't going in on that after all you boys done been there. What I had the first night will have to do for me."

"Well, I got some this morning and it weren't too bad," retorted Randy.

"Yea, but I got principles!" said Sam and with that, the three men started laughing.

Sam was still laughing at his joke as he walked across the camp to where his wounded man, Jeff Coleman, lay. Jeff had ridden with Sam for three years during the war and considered himself a good friend of the Roger family. Jeff was wrapped up in his blanket, his body shaking with fever. Sam knelt and pulling the blanket down, and began to remove the bloody bandage from Jeff's shoulder.

"That fella in town plugged me good. I'm gon'a need a doc here soon, Sam. Maybe Randy and I can slip back to Plano and see one there."

Sam got the bandage off and saw that the wound had festered up black, with yellow pus oozing from the hole and vicious red streaks radiated out and across Jeff's shoulder and down his chest.

"Man, Jeff, you done got you a first-class mess here. Ugly it is. Well, I guess it won't do no harm now to tell you who done kilt you. It was that Craig Mullins."

Jeff's eyes opened wide with surprise and he started to speak, but Sam gently put his hand over Jeff's mouth.

"Shhhhh! Now don't go getting all riled up. Yep, the same old Craig Mullins we use to ride with and whose ranch we visited. It was him and his big ass buddy, Jed Chance that threw down on us at the bank. Chance did for Jim and Frank. Man, that Jed can surely shoot, can't he?"

At the mention of Jed's name, Jeff's eyes widened further, and he started to speak, but again Sam stopped him.

"Now, friend, we got no doc and — Jeff, you done got the blood poison in' ya. So, here's how it's gon'a go."

And with that Sam clamped hard down on Jeff's mouth and drawing his knife he cut Jeff's throat with a quick slash that severed artery and windpipe.

Quickly standing and jumping back, "Damn Jeff! You have done shot blood all over my pants leg!" said Sam, as Jeff's boot heels drummed the ground as his life rushed out with the spurting blood.

Moments later, Sam threw the blanket over Jeff's lifeless body, stood and turned to find his brothers standing and staring at him. They had heard what he said to Coleman.

"What? He was done for anyway. I just hurried things along a bit!"

"Ain't that, Sam, it's just you never told us that it was Craig and Cap'n Chance in Dallas!" said a clearly agitated Bob Rogers.

"Yea, well, didn't want to get you boys all lathered up. Jed done growed his self a mustache, but it was him."

Randy Rogers stared at his big brother a moment then turning towards where the rest of the men who were slowly arranging their clothes and strapping on their gun belts, he yelled, "Get your asses moving! Get saddled up now! We is sitting leather in five minutes, so move!"

"Now, don't get all wadded up, Randy," said Sam. "They's back in Dallas, they ain't' gon'a be taking out after us."

"How do you know?" asked Bob Rogers, "Those two could come riding in here any minute!"

"Naw, they got no issue with us. Weren't their money we stole and 'sides Craig has that worn out ranch with the woman and boy to see too. Naw, they got no dog in this fight."

Sam stood there looking at his two brothers, hearing his own words but also remembering times past and those two men, and particularly Jed Chance and the things he had seen Jed do.

"You heard Randy. Get loaded up, now!" Sam yelled at the men. "Rio, put out that fire. Where's Spanish Bob?"

Rio, was a tall wiry man, dressed in black with

dark hair and pinched face that no matter how hard you might wash it, always looked grimy, and a mouth populated by dirty, yellow teeth. He wore a Concho studded gun belt slung low on his hip. He laughingly replied, "He's still at the girl. He does love the women!"

Sam turned to Randy, "Get Little Luke and you two get on our back trail. Go back a few miles, wait a day then start drifting back to us, but keep a watch for someone following. You see anyone, you come a running. And if you see that damn Jed Chance and Mullins on the hunt, don't, by God, try and take 'em yourself! We're going to hit that stream yonder and head south. We'll jump out of the water a mile or so down and head for Lampasas. We'll hold up with the Horrell boys til things get quiet. Mart owes me so should be no problem. After a bit, we'll move west and find some Comanche to sell that dark-haired bitch to and get safe passage through to New Mexico territory. Am I clear little brother?"

"Yea, I got'cha, I know what you want me to do. Still and all, if it is Chance and Mullins and I have a clear shot—"

Gripping his brother's arm, "Don't think about it Randy! We take those boys, we take them as a group," Sam said. "Now, get moving!"

With that said, Sam headed for the stand of trees where the older girl, Rose, had been dragged two nights ago and arrived in time to see Spanish Bob pulling up his pants and tucking himself away all the while looking at the still form of the girl on the ground.

"Bob, we got no more time. We got to move."

Bob was a big man with big belly and dark, coarse hair covering his arms and face. When he smiled, his arrangement of teeth looked something like a picket fence due to every other tooth being missing. No one knew why he was called Spanish Bob because he wasn't Spanish. He was born of white parents in the Oklahoma territory some twenty-nine years ago and managed to avoid serving on either side in the war.

Bob toed at the still body on the ground with his boot and told Sam, "She's got no buck in her anymore, Sam. The first couple of night, whoopee! She bucked like a mule with a fire up its ass, scratching and bite'n but now, nothing. You might as well be sticking ya dick in a cow's liver."

"Get on over to the camp and get saddled up. We're moving," Sam said as he looked down at the girl. She was a sight. He kneeled next to her as Spanish Bob moved toward the camp. Her once pretty face was swollen from repeated blows and her nose was bent and broken. Her blue eyes were nearly swollen shut, her body was a mass of cuts and bruises, one nipple was nearly bitten through and other bite marks were scattered about her body. She had a few burns on her where someone, probably Rio, had used a heated knife on her. Her inner thighs were a bloody mess.

"Damn girl! You should 'a been more cooperative." As Sam spoke, Rose turned her head toward him and a low moan escaped her lips. She wanted to raise her hands to him, to plead for mercy, for no more, no more.

"Well, you just a waste now girl, and a distraction I don't need. I got to have my boys focused."

Sam stood from where he had been kneeling next to Rose and placed his boot on her throat. Rose looked at him, knowing, and in a last burst of desperate strength tried to remove his boot from its place. She clawed with broken nails at the leather, pushing at it with her last bit of strength, but she could not move it. She needed to live, not just for herself but for Katherine!

Sam said, "Sorry, girlie." And with that, he pressed down on her throat and moved his weight over her so in a moment the full of his two hundred pounds crushed her into the ground. After two or three minutes, he removed his boot and turned to start back toward the camp when he thought he heard a sigh or some noise from the brutalized girl.

"Damn, you are a tough one." He kicked her hard in the side of the head, once, twice, three times. Sam Rogers turned from Rose's lifeless body and walked back into camp.

Chapter 11

Jed and Craig had ridden hard for most of four days. They had found the spot where the posse had been ambushed and easily picked up the trail of the outlaws. Jed was very pleased with his new horse. She moved with a smooth gait and had quick feet. The mare had no problem carrying him and his supplies. She probably wasn't the fastest of horses, but he liked her bulk and strength.

Each morning upon rising Craig watched Jed practice with his guns. Drawing and spinning 'round, drawing from a crouch, drawing, and drawing, and drawing, for twenty or so minutes he did this. Craig marveled at his friend's speed and agility.

The outlaws had been on the run for almost four days when Jed and Craig had started out. The two pursuers were pushing it hard. They knew that two could move a lot faster than the group of outlaws. They had crossed the Brazos River and Craig figured they were near Palo Pinto or there about. The two friends didn't know how hard the outlaws were pushing it but knew that for the sake of the two girls they had to move fast. They stayed in the saddle as much as possible and ate and slept little. Ten or so white men traveling in a group can't move through the plains without leaving a trail and the two friends followed it each day until it was too dark to see.

On the fourth night, they made camp on a knoll covered in tall grass and wildflowers. It was a cold camp and they dined on dried beef, a can of beans and water from their canteens. They hobbled their horses and after feeding their mounts oats and watering them, the men lay down to catch some sleep.

They came charging through the tall grass running fast and bent over, long guns firing. Their blue clothes so dirty and dusty they looked like the Gray of the Confederacy. They yelled and came on despite the bullets hitting them! Cannon fire raked their lines but on they came! Suddenly, they're eyes disappeared, just holes draining blood but on they came! Craig fell back in the trench, he tried to raise his gun, but it was too heavy he couldn't move it! Now they were on him only their guns disappeared, and they reached for him with bloody hands, hands that turned into razor sharp bayonets! They were stabbing him! Stabbing and stabbing and....!

"Wake up! Wake up Craig! Wake up!" Jed implored his friend as he roughly shook his shoulder.

"What—I— they was—!"

"Just a dream, Craig, just a bad dream is all. It's ok now."

Jed had observed Craig's fitful sleep each night and he realized his friend was having a hard time with something. He wouldn't pry; he would let Craig tell it in his own time. Seeing that his friend was fully awake, Jed moved back to his blanket and lay down.

Craig, his face sweaty and flushed was restless and truthfully didn't want to go back to sleep. He didn't want to have the dream again. He thought of Ruth and Jeff and missed them a lot.

"Hey, Jed?"

"Yea?"

"Just wondering, you think you'll marry again?"

"Pard, it's a weird time to be asking me that what with what we got going on right now," said Jed as he settled himself down.

"I know, but I got Ruth and the boy on my mind and sure do miss 'em. And I was just wondering is all."

"No, no plans on that right now. And if you want to keep breathing you better get your head empty of those two and working on the chore we got in front of us."

"I know, I know. Hey, what did you and Mrs. Henderson converse on 'fore we rode out? Seemed like some secret talk to me."

"Well, she wanted me to promise her something. She wanted me to promise her that if the girls are dead or, you know, messed up — that I would kill the outlaws, down to the last man."

"Wow! That lady ain't to be trifled with. Got some meanness in her I believe."

"Yea, she's got grit that's for sure."

"So, what did you tell her?"

"Told her I would, I'll kill every mother's son of them."

After a moment of silence, Craig asked, "Can you do that, Jed? Are you that good? I mean, I know what a hellion you were on the battlefield and I seen you do some things — well, anyway that was war and all so, can you do it?"

After a moment of hesitation, "Yea, yea I can do it. Killing—well, killing has always been easy for me. The thing is, when it's happening everything just seems to slow down. I just seem to know who and where to shoot and they all just seem so slow, leastways to me it seems that way. So, yes, I can do it. Besides Pard, I got you there to help. It'll be a barn dance."

Craig chuckled and sarcastically said, "Yea, a barn dance with the Rogers boys. Sounds like a fun time for all."

"Yea, now settle down friend and let's get some sleep," said Jed.

And with that, the two friends drifted off to sleep. One slept with no dreams to disturb his slumber, while the other tossed and turned, remembering the horrors of the past war and the battles fought and the men he had killed visited his dreams.

Slightly less than a mile west of where Jed and Craig bedded down, in a dry, shallow wash, Randy Rogers and Little Luke McCoy were bedding down. McCoy was a skinny, nervous little man, with a scraggly beard but not much hair on his head, but good with a gun and brother of Big Luke McCoy, both born and raised in Shreveport, Louisiana. The parents of Little Luke and

Big Luke were among the laziest of folks. They were so lazy that when their second son came along they endowed him with the same name as their first child, so they did not have to try and think of another name. The two men had back trailed, just like Sam had said do, and were intending to start drifting back in the direction of the other outlaws at first light. They also were working a cold camp.

"I'm a telling you Randy, I gots a feeling and you knowed how when I gets a feeling 'bout some thing you know it pert' almost be a'happ'n. You'd known since the war 'bout them feelings I git and I gots one now, we got trouble close by, I tell 'ya!"

"All right, all right, just shut up would ya? You done been going on 'bout your goddamn feelings for most of the day, now, shut up or ya going to feel my boot up your skinny ass, ya here?" With that, Randy pulled his blanket up and resting his head on his saddle tried to get some sleep.

"Well," whispered Little Luke McCoy of Shreveport, La., as he turned over and closed his eyes, "I gots a feeling anyway."

Daybreak and in the camp of the pursuers and they fed on corn dodgers and beef jerky. Craig talked

Chance into letting him start a small fire to heat some water for coffee.

In the camp of the bad men, they fed on similar fare and after their morning constitutionals began saddling up. Randy Rogers was just starting to cinch up his mare when...

"Think I seen smoke."

"What 'cha say?" asked Randy as he turned and saw Little Luke staring off toward the east.

"Smoke, thought I saw some, like a puff of a fire."

"Damn, Little L, you are a jumpy one. Get saddled and let's get moving." Randy pulled himself into the saddle and as he pulled his horse around...

"Damn! Seen it! Seen it too! It was just a puff but damn if it weren't smoke. There be someone on our trail for sure!"

"Want to sneak over to their way and see who it is?" asked Little Luke as he absent-mindedly loosened his gun from his holster, over and over.

"Hell no, could be a passel of posse boys, Luke!"

After a few moments of pondering the situation, Randy said, "Tell ya what. Let's move back to that rocky hill we passed late yesterday. We could spy out who it is trailing us from there."

"Sounds good, Randy. I'm all for it."

And with that Little Luke mounted up and the two men turned and rode.

Chance and Craig had finished their meager breakfast and coffee and as Craig put the fire out with water from his canteen...

"Damn! Poured that water too fast and made the fire smoke up! Hope it weren't seen."

Jed didn't respond as he just stood by his saddled horse, looking to the west.

"Course, if they did see it maybe it would make 'em nervous and they wouldn't be thinking 'bout the girls."

Jed turned and said to his friend, "They done had those girls for six days and nights with no posse putting pressure on them to make them nervous and to keep 'em moving. I fear those men have had plenty of time to get at those girls. I think those girls are done for."

Neither man spoke as they finished breaking camp and headed west. In an hour or so they came to a wash where they moved south and after traveling a distance—

"Horse apples."

Craig was leading their pack horse and coming up on Jed asked, "What 'cha say?"

"Horseshit. Droppings over in that grassy area yonder," Jed said as he motioned to his left, "and the grass is pressed down in places where horses laid down. And look, here in the wash, boot prints, looks like low heel Calvary boots, of two men, one big, one smallish."

Craig dismounted and poked at the horse dropping with a stick, "Got some heat in em, Jed. They be kind 'a fresh. I think maybe just two or three hours since they was dropped."

"I think it was some of our robbers," said Jed. "You remember how we use to get the boys to back trail to check for those blue boys trying to sneak up on us? I think that's what we got here. Two men, cold camp, yea, I think it's them. Sam ain't dumb. He'd do something like that."

Craig looked around, worry lines creasing his brow. He moved quickly to his scabbard and pulled his Winchester and levered a round into the chamber. His horse, sensing Craig's nervousness stamped and snorted prompting Craig to grab the reins tighter.

"Whoa Pard, if they was still here they would have done for us already. Settle down, and calm that pony down too," said Jed.

Jed dismounted and studied the ground around the cold camp closely. His friend's behavior was a little troublesome and he, from the corner of his eye, watched Craig. Craig had always been dependable when the chips were down, and things got tough, but his nervousness was bothersome to Jed.

"Craig, friend, are you ok? You seem, well, not yourself; never seen you jumpy like this before and, well, with that dream last night and all I—"

"Yea" replied Craig as he laughed nervously. "Just, uh, well, it's been awhile since I was up against trouble, you know. Guess I'm out of practice. I'll be ok, just got to get my soldier legs again."

"You thinking you might have made a mistake getting us all committed to getting those girls back?"

"No, no, I'll be fine Jed and taking Mrs. Henderson's offer was best for us, you and me and Ruth and Jeff too. It'll all work out and I'll be ok. I won't let you down, promise."

Jed smiled at his friend, "I know you won't Pard. You've always come through in a pinch and fight'n ain't no stranger to you neither. You'll be fine. Now, let's move on real watchful like. I think them Rogers boys have fallen back on our old tricks of sending men to check the back trail. 'Course might be they was just stragglers but let's be on guard. Let's move forward one on each side of this trail they left, 'bout fifteen yards or so between us so we ain't bunched up."

With that, Jed mounted up and shucked his Winchester from its scabbard and after checking the action for dirt, he levered a round into the chamber. The two friends rode onward, watchful and alert for danger but moving as fast as possible because they both knew without saying it that if the outlaws knew they were in close pursuit the girls were in real danger, if they were still alive. They moved at pace, studying the ground and scanning the horizon for danger. It was there.

Chapter 12

The sun rises in the east, sets in the west. Everyone knows that. It's taught in school but even if it wasn't, you would know. Just living life, you would know, but knowing and remembering is, well, different. Forgetting something so simple can be a dangerous thing, particularly on the outlaw trail.

It was almost noon, the sun almost fully overhead, almost. Randy Rogers and Little Luke McCoy lay on a rocky hill, probably no more than a hundred paces up from the prairie floor, their bellies pressed as hard as possible into the prairie grass, lying as low as possible. McCoy had pulled his Sharps 50-90 from his saddle and had the long-barreled rifle cocked and ready. McCoy had used the rifle to shoot blue coats at long range during the war and was a good shot. He almost never missed, almost never.

It's ten or so minutes to high noon and the two bad men could see the two horsemen following their trail. They had been watching the growing figures for several minutes and Little Luke McCoy asked for about the hundredth time, "Well, damn, is it them? Is it?" His fingers nervously fingered his rifle's stock.

"Not sure, I think so but not sure. That big guy on the right could be Chance. Not sure, though," said Randy Rogers.

"Hell man! Put the glass on 'em again! See who they be!"

It's about seven minutes to high noon.

Randy thought about it a minute, two, then picked up his spyglass, taken from a dead union officer years ago and glassed the two riders coming from the east, east to west, not yet high noon, five till.

"Pull up there, Pard," called out Chance," Seems my cinch is loose." And with that, Jed dismounted and casually turned his mare's head across their intended path, putting his horse between him and the waiting outlaws.

"Hey Craig, move over here. Shuck your ass from that saddle and walk toward me but do it casual like."

Craig did just that, leading his horse and the pack animal to where Jed was tugging on his saddle,

"What's up?"

"'bout a hundred yards or so directly in front of us is a knoll, got some rock and mesquite on top. Somebody was glassing us. I saw the reflection off the glass when the sun hit it. It's got to be our two back trailing outlaws."

Craig turned to the pack animal and pulled a canteen and as he drank he let his eyes scan the knoll. "Yep, think I saw a smudge of movement. It was brief but pretty sure it was there. Whatcha want to do?"

"Get down, you damn fool!" said Randy as he grabbed Little Luke McCoy by his gun belt and pulled him back to his belly. "It's them damn it! Chance and Mullins! Damn it to hell! Why'd it have to be them? Man, that fucking Chance, that son of a bitch!"

"I just eased up a little, just getting a quick look, that's all, they sure didn't see me, and I'm small, ain't no way they seen me!"

"Shut up and let me think!"

"Let my Sharps reach out to 'em, Randy! I can get 'em. Pick that Chance off clean I will!"

"You don't shut up I'm going to gut you and leave you here!" blurted a nervous and scared Randy Rogers as he pulled his knife on Little Luke McCoy.

"Ok, ok, relax, Randy, relax and I'll shut up."

Randy closed his eyes and thought about what do to. He pinched his nose, furrowed his brow and breathed slow, deep breaths, thinking, and thinking. Without changing position, he spoke to Little Luke McCoy, "Ok. What are they doing now?"

Little Luke McCoy eased his head up and looked to where Jed and Craig had stopped, "Well, Randy, they—they ain't there now."

"What the fuck, Luke?" and Randy raised his head and looked toward the plains—empty.

"Where the hell—there! Look there, 'bout fifty yards or so south of where they were. Must be a little draw there covered with grass, I suppose, so makes it hard to see. I see a horse's rear end just sticking out. That's where they are! See 'em, Luke?"

"There's a horse's ass sticking out? Which one, Chance or Mullins?" asked a chuckling Little Luke Mc-Coy.

"Shut up, Luke!" said Randy but he couldn't suppress a smile, "'sides, could be either!"

And both men had to smile.

The two outlaws were still smiling three of four minutes later when—

"What the hell? You smell that, Luke? They done started a fire, a campfire. Them two fools are nooning right now in that draw."

"Let's do for 'em, Randy! We can do it, me and you, and take their heads back for Sam to see."

"Hold on, Luke. Moving on those two can't be done lightly. Sam said his own self that you could stick a knife in Jed's heart and it would still take him ten minutes to die and he'd be killing 'ya the whole time."

"Uh, what's that mean, Randy?"

"That he's a tough man to kill, Luke, tough to kill, but, still and all, he's a man and put enough lead in 'em, he'll die like any other man."

Randy was beginning to warm to the idea of sneaking up on the two men while they were having their noon break. Taking their heads back to Sam would surely please his brothers and would raise his own stock in both his brothers' eyes and with the other men too.

"What we gon'a do, Randy? What we—"

"Luke, shut your mouth and listen. They gon'a be eat'n and taking a piss break for maybe thirty minutes or so. We gon'a snake down there through this here grass like we snuck on those blue boys in the war, and we gon'a kill those two bastards right proper. Make Sam proud, it will. Now, keep quiet and follow me."

"Right, Randy, right with ya!"

The two outlaws raised themselves to a crouch and began to move forward when—

"Now, hold on boys, don't run off."

The two bad men quickly turned, and there stood Jed and Craig. Craig carried his scatter gun held loosely across his body, his right hand on the stock. To his left stood Jed, his right hand hanging a few inches from his Colt, loose, waiting.

Randy and Little Luke McCoy struggled to get over the shock of the two men standing there on their little hill. Randy's hand rested on the butt of his Smith &Wesson #3, worn cross draw, and little Luke McCoy was still holding his Sharps rifle, pointed at the ground but in line with Jed.

For a minute, the four men just looked at each other. The breeze moved the Buffalo Grass, rustled the mesquite. A lone Mockingbird made to land in the brush but decided to seek safer shelter. For a few moments, save the wind, all was quiet on the little knoll, quiet and peaceful.

"Well, now, ain't this a right fandango," said Randy, as he recovered his wits, "We saw you boys down in that little draw and was just going down to pay our respects and such. We—uh, we're just out looking for cattle and—Uh—"

"Where's the girls, Randy?" asked Jed.

"Well, I don't rightly know what you're speaking on Jed, but my, I think you might be a tad bigger than when I last saw you, boy!"

"'Bout the same, I think. Now, where are the girls, Randy?"

"Well, how'd you two—"

"You glassed us, saw the glass reflect when the sun hit it. You should have waited till the sun got behind 'ya, but, well, you never was the smart one of you Rogers boys. We left our horses in a little draw but, so you could see em, started a little fire and used that little draw to come up behind you two," said Jed.

As the two men talked, Little Luke McCoy was taking stock of the situation. His Sharps was just inches away from being able to gut shoot Chance, just inches. Maybe, four inches he thought, six at the most. Just a quick tilt up and pull the trigger, then Randy could take Mullins. Randy was quick, always had been quick. Just a few inches, four, six at the most, just up and shoot, up and shoot. So, he did exactly that, quickly up and...

Jed's first bullet caught Little Luke two inches below his left nipple, blowing out a sizable chunk of flesh as the big slug exited his back and began a journey across the prairie to eventually fall to the ground. The job it had been made for many months ago done.

Little Luke McCoy had just a twinkling of a moment to ponder just how many inches he had managed to raise his Sharps before Jed 's second bullet blew apart his heart and severed his spinal cord on its way out. Little Luke McCoy, late of Shreveport, Louisiana, fell dead.

Randy had noted the tension in Luke's body and knew he was about to make a move and when he sensed Luke's play he pulled his gun, determined to end Jed and Craig, now!

That thought was still passing through his brain and his noise maker was just clearing leather when Jed 's third shot hit him, low, about three inches below his navel and spun him like a top and he flopped down on the rocks behind him.

The three shots were almost as one, as they were so fast and so close together. Jed stood, gun smoking, looking at the two men, one dead, the other moaning and spurting blood, dying, but slowly.

Jed glanced at Craig and asked, "You ok, Pard?"

Craig didn't answer. Jed looked over at him. Craig's shotgun had never moved, and his hands were shaking, just a bit, but shaking.

"Son of a bitch, Jed, I mean—damn!"

Turning slightly towards his friend but keeping his eyes on the dying Randy Rogers, "Its ok, Craig. Now, how 'bout going down and put out that fire and get our animals and bring them on up. I'm going to talk with Randy here while he's still breathing."

A shaken Craig moved off to get the horses while Jed knelt next to the dying outlaw.

"You're done for, Randy. I shot you in the gut on purpose, so you'd die slow and hurt'n. Now, I can make it quick or I can just leave you here dying slow like. Tell me where the girls are. Where'd you bastards leave their bodies?"

Randy's guts burned like fire and he writhed on the ground, trying to find relief that wasn't going to come until he was dead.

"Fuck you, Jed! You done killed me. I ain't gon'a tell you nothing!"

"Fine, Randy," Jed said as he stood up, "just lay here and die then, maybe you'll be dead 'for the wolves and coyotes start to hunt this evening."

"Wait, wait a damn minute!"

Randy had seen men die gut shot and it some-times would take days of pain and agony for the man before merciful death.

"Don't leave me like this, Jed! End it for me. We rode together, you owe me that!"

"Where are the girls?'

"Don't know now — ugh, hurts something awful! The youngest one was fine last time I seen her, 'bout two days ago — the other — the other girl," and he looked up at Jed and smiled, "well — damn — she was entertaining the boys at camp. I had me a slice or two myself 'fore — "

Whatever Randy was going to say was cut off by the pain shooting through his belly and he moaned and writhed looking for relief.

Jed's features were cold and unreadable as he stared at the dying outlaw at his feet,

"Where?"

"Bout twelve or fifteen miles south — a — a long side a wide creek — in — shit! I'm hurting Jed!"

"Where?"

"In a grove — by that creek, now do for me now Jed, you said — you said you would!"

Jed could hear Craig coming up with their horses and he knelt and picked up Randy's pistol, broke it open, dropped shells from it, then dropped it in the dirt by Randy's side.

"Here, I left you one round. You do yourself."

"Fuck you, Jed! Them boys is headed for Lampasas then west to find some Comanche to sell the youngest girl too. I'm telling 'ya so you can catch up to 'em, Jed! I'm telling 'ya so Sam can kill you! Sam—Sam, he's gon'a kill you dead, you—bastard!"

"You'll never know, boy."

And with that, Jed moved off down the slope to where Craig was waiting.

"I found their mounts hobbled down here at the base of the hill and pulled their saddles and turned them loose. Didn't see we had a need for 'em. How's Randy?"

"He's dead."

"We gon'a bury them boys?"

Jed turned to Craig and the look in his eyes was such that Craig took a step back.

"I made a promise to Mrs. Henderson. I intend to keep it."

"Ok, Jed, your call."

"Let's split what we can carry off that pack horse and turn it loose. We got to move fast. Randy says the girls were 'bout ten miles or so south in a grove, next to a wide creek. We got to move, now!"

The two men quickly took what they needed from their pack horse and left the rest there on the ground and turned the horse loose. Maybe it would make its way back to the Henderson ranch but probably not. That was a long way away.

They mounted and spurred their mounts south, but both men knew there was a talk coming on what happened with Craig on the hill.

A gut shot man dies slowly. His life leaks out and pools around him on the ground. It's a painful, agonizing death. Thirst and pain fought like raging beast within Randy Rogers. He needed just one drink, just one taste of sweet, cool water, and he needed relief from the fierce pain in his belly that burned with the fires of hell!

He lay there for hours, his life oozing out around him. Consciousness came and went. He fought the pain but couldn't get the courage to end it all. Hours passed. It grew dark and the hour late and the critters came out. He heard shuffling at the base of the hill. There was something pacing around the hill, a growl from a hungry throat and the snapping of powerful jaws, one, no two of 'em, maybe more! The minutes past, ten, then twenty, now there was more than one or two and only the man smell keeping em from coming. He had to do it now!

Randy reached for his gun and with a blood crusted hand, thumbed back the hammer and placed the barrel under his chin, thinking, "I hope Sam kills Jed slow, makes him suffer. Damn his soul!"

With that thought, he pulled the trigger —

Nothing!

He quickly pulled the hammer back and again pulled the trigger. Nothing!

"Damn him! Damn Jed to hell! He didn't leave a bullet for me!"

The wolves came in a rush.

A day and a half ride south Sam Rogers and his band were moving toward Lampasas. Katherine Henderson sat astride her mount, softly crying. She didn't want the men to hear her because when they did one of them would ride by and punch her arm or give her head a shove or slap. Hopelessness and sadness were constant companions. When the group had mounted up and left the clearing by the creek, Rose didn't join them. No one had told her, but she knew from what she overheard that her sister was dead. Katherine felt nothing but despair. She mourned her sister and mourned for herself. She was lost and alone and didn't know what would happen to her but lived in fear of the men killing her too, but she was a Henderson and she was determined to face whatever was coming as bravely as possible.

Chapter 13

Jed and Craig moved as quickly as possible through the buffalo grass and occasional stand of juniper and oak trees. Randy and Little Luke had not done much to hide their trail so it was that late in the afternoon they spotted the grove they believed that Randy Rogers had spoken of. A hundred yards of so out from the grove they dismounted and taking their Winchesters, moved in a skirmish line toward the grove. It wasn't too long before the men smelled the scent of death coming from the trees. A stench they were both familiar with. Jed stopped and looked at Craig, twenty or so yards to his right.

"They ain't here, Pard. They moved on."

"You think?"

"Ain't no right in the head man gon'a stay in that place with that smell keep'n him company. No, no way."

"Yea, you got a point there."

The friends moved on to the grove. They entered from the north side. Straight away, they came upon Jeff Coleman's body, still lying under his blanket. Being in the grove not many of the critters had gotten to the body, except a few beetles, flies, ants and a mouse or two.

Pulling the blanket back, "Craig, he looked familiar to ya?"

"Little, but damn, he's so swole up it's hard to say, but does look familiar, though," said Craig, as he pulled his kerchief up over his nose to try to ward off the smell.

"I think this is the one you dusted back during the robbery. Looks like a right shoulder wound and that surely is where you hit 'em. I'm pretty sure it's Coleman, Jeff Coleman. He rode with us the last year or two of the war." said Jed.

Yea, remember him, Jed. He should 'a chose another line of work, I reckon."

"Yep, other friends too, looks like someone cut this throat."

Craig moved on toward the abandoned camp area while Jed moved toward the creek.

Craig was kicking at the camp fire remains when Jed called out,

"Here, she's here."

"What? What"cha say?"

"The oldest girl, Rose, the blonde one, she's here."

Craig moved toward the sound of Jed's voice and found him by the creek in a little stand of cottonwood saplings. He was standing, hat in his hand, over the now ugly and decomposing body of Rose Henderson.

Even with the current state of the body, both men knew she had suffered mightily at the end of her life. The burns, cut marks, and bruising were still evident, and they could see the right side of her head had been crushed. Her bloody thighs told them all they needed to know about her last hours on earth.

Craig removed his hat and his eyes burned both from the smell and the emotion of the moment. He looked at this friend and saw no emotion on his face, but Jed's eyes burned with a fire.

"Jed, I—"

"I'll bury her, Craig. I'll scout out a good place for her to rest. A place her grandma can find and take her back home, if she's a mind to do that."

"I can help you. Let me—"

"Craig, just get the horses down here and get my rain slicker and the shovel. I'll scout out a spot to lay her down."

Craig moved off toward the camp and when he glanced back he saw his friend kneeling by the body of the young girl. Jed was talking to her in a soothing, quiet voice as his big hand stroked her blood matted and filthy hair. Craig could not hear what Jed said to the girl, and he never asked. A short while later Craig returned with the horses. Jed came from the creek and got his slicker.

"You find a place?"

"Yea, I'd say it's a nice place. It's just a mite north of this spot, 'bout a hundred yards or so."

Both men moved to where Rose lay and as Jed knelt and began wrapping her in his slicker, Craig couldn't help but notice how gentle Jed was with her. He noticed that Jed's lips moved in a whispered conversation as if he was speaking to her.

Jed easily picked up the body and began working his way along the creek, through the patches of brush and around the oaks, elms, and pecan trees. Craig, following along behind, noticed that Jed didn't appear at all bothered by the smell of the decomposing body.

After a distance, Jed moved toward the bank and pushed through a particularly thick stand of brush and briars and Craig, moving behind him, pushed through also and suddenly the brush ended and Craig could see they were on a finger of the creek bank, about forty or so feet wide, sticking out into the water. At the end of the finger, above the flowing creek, grew a tall, stately oak. This finger of the bank was about twenty feet above the water level. The water moved by the spot quiet and slow. A Jay squawked from the oak tree, a bright red Cardinal flew in and out of the brush and from the thick woods across the creek Craig could hear squirrels in an argument over nuts or maybe a mate. Despite all that, it was peaceful. It was an ideal resting place for one who had died so violently.

Jed gently laid the body down; he stripped off his shirt and taking the shovel from Craig he began to dig Rose's grave under the branches of the old oak.

For an hour or so Craig watched his friend dig. Jed didn't tire. His heavily muscled shoulders and arms shined with sweat in the fading light of day as he scooped out shovel loads of dark, rich soil. After a time, Jed stopped shoveling, looked around and said, "Think this should do it. How 'bout you, what'd you think?"

"Mighty fine, Jed, looks good to me."

Jed reached for Rose's body where it lay next to the hole and lifted and lowered her into it. He whispered to her as he lay her down, "You rest easy right here, Miss Rose. Nobody's gon'a bother you, not anymore. Rest easy and directly I'll fetch your grandma here to see you. I'll get your sister, Rose, and I will do justice for you on those that hurt you, all of them, to a man. This I swear to you, so rest now. Be at peace."

Jed climbed from the grave, filled it and tamping down the mound of earth he turned to Craig, "Pard, I would like your help fetching some rock up from the creek to cover her spot here."

"Well, sure Jed, let's do it."

So, the men found an animal trail down to the creek and making repeated trips covered Rose's grave with large, smooth, flat river rocks.

When they finished Jed said, "Craig, I'm gon'a go wash up in the creek. I won't be long then you can get washed up too. Then we'll move away a bit to get shed of the smell of Jeff back yonder."

"Sure Jed, but don't be too long. I don't cotton to sitting there breathing his stink."

Craig had been back where he had left the horses about twenty minutes or so when Jed showed up. His hair and clothes damp from his washing. Craig went and did his cleaning up and returned.

The men mounted, but before moving off Jed turned to Craig and said, "Craig, if I don't make it, fetch Mrs. Henderson here to see Rose. Might be she would want to leave her here but maybe she wants her closer to home. Would ya do that?"

"Sure, Jed, I'll do it, but you know you're gon'a —"

"Alright then, that's settled," Jed interrupted, "Now, just where about do you figure we are, Craig? "

"Well," said Craig, scratching at his growth of beard and looking around at the terrain, "I'd say we are somewhat south to Palo Pinto and that creek yonder is some part of Leon Creek, leastways, that's how I figure it."

Jed pondered on it a minute then said, "Let's move off a bit and make camp. Randy said his brother was taking the other girl, Katherine, to Lampasas and then west to sell her to the Comanche. We'll camp, sleep a bit, and then hit the trail."

And with that, the two men spurred their mounts toward the south and Lampasas, Texas.

Chapter 14

After traveling a few miles or so and with darkness about full on, Jed and Craig reined in. They took care of their horses and built a fire for coffee and beans from they're dwindling supplies. Jed cleaned his .45 after supper and then the two friends settled in for a few hours sleep, but before drifting off...

"Jed, uh, I think we need to talk about today. You know, with Little Luke and Randy and what happened on that hill."

"Nothing to talk 'bout, Craig, it's over, nothing to speak on at all," said Jed as he adjusted his saddle to use as a pillow.

"I—I just froze up, Jed. I—it—well, in town during the shooting and all it was so fast I didn't have time to think but out here, on that hill—I just", Craig stood and began pacing. "I just froze. Killing—I just don't know if— "

Jed lay down on his blanket, staring at the stars.

"Craig, let it go. When the time is right, you'll be there for me. I guarantee it."

Craig moved to the dying fire, just embers now, tested the coffee pot but found it empty. He moved back to his blanket and lay down.

"The blood dreams — I get the blood dreams. Do you get 'em, Jed?"

Rolling onto his elbow Jed looked at his friend, "Don't know what you mean, Pard. What's a blood dream?"

"Dreams of the fighting and the men you killed in the war, blood dreams. Least ways that's what Ruth calls 'em. The men you killed in the war, they're always there when you close your eyes, always staring at 'ya, coming for 'ya, always bloody!" Clearly agitated, Craig had moved to his knees, he was staring at the ground as if seeing something there and rubbing his thighs, his breathing heavy. "I just seem to always have 'em. You, you have 'em too, doesn't ya Jed?"

Jed knew, from the war and his experiences both before and after, that each man deals with killing and death in his own way. Some men run from it and it haunts them forever, others embrace it, had even sought it out. Still others, like him, accepted it, put it in its place

116

and moved on, never to think on it again unless he needed to for some reason. Jed knew his friend was having a bad time of it but he didn't know what to do for him, how to ease his mind.

"No, Craig. I don't have bloody dreams or dreams of killing at all. What we did, we did. It don't make me happy but it don't bother me neither. We fought for something. I guess each man a different thing in his own mind, I don't rightly know but I know we didn't just kill to be killing. It was a war."

"I know you think I done gone soft and I—"

"Stop it, Craig!" Jed's voice rose. "Stop it now! You ain't soft at all! I fought with you, I seen what you done in war and 'sides soft men don't take up a woman and boy and try to scratch out a living on a dirt ranch in Texas. You ain't soft and I ain't gon'a tolerate you saying otherwise!"

The two friends just stared at each other for a moment. Jed had never raised his voice to Craig and Craig was a little shocked by his friend's anger.

Tamping down his anger, Jed said, "Now, listen Craig, we did what we did in the war 'cause that's what we was ordered to do. You didn't kill no man that wasn't trying to kill you. You, me, even the men we killed had a

117

reason to be there, no matter what it was. We did what we were told but each man was there for his own reason, his own calling. You didn't kill kids, women or unarmed men. You kilt men trying to do for you. That's it."

"Ok, Jed, ok. I'm just upset that I didn't pull my weight back there with Luke and Randy is all it is."

"Craig, you just watch my back and I'll do all the killing that needs to be done. Just don't let me get back shot and all will be good. 'Sides, think back on it, today on the knoll. When Little Luke set off that party, did you have time to gets that coach gun working?"

Craig thought about the shooting and how it went down. So fast, just so damn fast!

"I—it was—it was over so quick. No, no, you were too fast. You had done shot 'em both before I could move."

"That's right, Pard. You didn't freeze. You were just slow. You got to work on that speed."

With that Jed lay back down and taking his .45 in his hand he rested it on his chest and closed his eyes. Within just a few deep breaths he was asleep and sleeping peacefully.

Craig looked at this big friend for a moment then lay down and closed his eyes. He tossed fitfully and

118

thought for a long time on the things his friend had said. Sleep finally came and so did the blood dreams, only tonight they weren't so bad and eventually faded away.

Chapter 15

Some four days later in the outlaw camp five miles outside of Lampasas in a clearing some fifty yards from a creek, and just after noon.

Sam and his brother, Bob, stood on the edge of camp, smoking and drinking coffee. Both men were staring off to the north, each lost in his own thoughts on their brother, Randy.

"He ain't coming, Bob."

"Don't know that, Sam. He could be—"

"No, I think he's dead and most likely Little Luke too. Otherwise, they would 'a done caught up with us. No, they ain't coming. Our little brother is dead. Could be he's done been caught, but more likely he's dead. He'd fight to the end, he would."

After a few moments of silence, Bob ground his smoke beneath the heel of his boot and said, "You think they'd talk, tell where we are going?"

Sam, dropping his smoke and taking his hat off

and wiping his brow with his sleeve said, "Don't know, don't rightly know, but could be. If'n it was a sheriff's posse or some soldier boys, then, no, I don't, but if'n it be Jed and Craig, well, I seen what Jed can do when he's riled, you have too so if it does happen to be them, then them boys talked. I been pondering it and maybe those two bastards hooked on with a sheriff's posse. You know, kind' a drafted in cause they knowed us. Don't know, but we got to be watchful. I got to get into town and look up the Horrell boys. Might be we don't hang 'round here as long as I figured on."

"Ok, but we need to get the boys into town too. They're tired of eat'n nothing but Pecos Strawberries and they are itching to spend some of that money we took and to check out some sport'n gals. We got 'a keep 'em off that girl yonder or we got nothing to trade to them injuns, so no safe passage for us."

"Ok, tell ya what. I'll take Rio and Jim into town with me and check things out, get with the Horrells, and we three will get leaned out with some whiskey and women. You stay here with the others and keep 'em off that girl yonder. We come back; you can take them into town to party while we stay here with the girl. We should be back by tomorrow, 'bout this time."

"Sounds good, Sam."

And with that, the two men moved off to put into action their plan. However, plans often don't work out like, well, like they were planned.

A few hours after Sam and his two companions had left their camp and about two hundred yards north of the outlaw camp, on the same side of the creek, Jed Chance and Craig Mullins reigned in their mounts.

"Hey, how close you figure we are to Lampasas?" asked Jed.

"Ummmm, I'm guessing not too far t'all. Maybe, uh, maybe two, three hours ride. We can make it by nightfall, I 'spect."

"Yea, I figure the same. Well, let's don't go riding in there at night. I heard Lampasas can be a tough town and maybe Sam and Bob got friends there. It's dark and they see us coming and we don't see them, well, things could get a might too tight for us. Let's set up camp here and ride in first thing in the morning. Might be we catch Sam and his bunch sleeping one off. Surely would make things easy for us if'n that was the case. 'Course, they may have already moved on or that damn Randy might have just outright lied 'bout where Sam and his bunch were going. We'll be careful just in case."

Jed and Craig stripped the saddles and supplies from their horses and Craig volunteered to take the horses down to the creek. Taking each horse by the reins, he set off to take care of that chore while Jed started a small fire to heat some coffee and rustle up some food.

A hundred yards of so south of where Craig was watering their mounts, Big Luke McCoy, older brother of Little Luke McCoy, now deceased, was watering the horses of the outlaw band when he heard a horse snort, once, twice. He stood in the knee-deep water holding the reins to the watering horses and stared off to the north. Maybe he was mistaken? Maybe just...nope, there it was again, another snort. Stray? Injuns? Nope, wouldn't be injuns this close to town. Dropping the reins, Big Luke pulled his Navy Colt and began to move quietly up the stream, staying close to the brushy bank, moving slow and easy.

Craig was watering the horses, thinking about Ruth. He had made up his mind that he was going to marry her as soon as they got back to Dallas. He was going to make an honest woman of her and they would — He turned quickly at the sound of a splash behind him! He found himself looking down the barrel of Big Luke's Colt, not fifteen feet away. Big Luke stood in the stream, with a big grin on his face.

"Well looky here! My, my I do declare if it ain't Mr. Craig Mullins. Craig, what the hell are you doing here so far from that ranch of yours? Get them hands up Craig, and keep 'em there, boy!" Big Luke's gun barrel never wavered. It was rock steady pointing at the center of Craig's chest.

Craig caught completely off guard, froze, not knowing exactly what to do but he quickly decided to try to hide the fact that Jed was close by.

Well, Big Luke, I was, uh, looking for you boys. Yea, I was looking for ya'll figure to join up like old times. I was tired of that ranch life anyway and — "

"Shut your face, Craig"

"Uh, now no need to — "

"I said shut up! You ain't here to join nobody. We knows it was you and Cap'n Chance that throwed down on us back in Dallas. Sam and Bob figured you two might be on our trail."

It suddenly dawned on Big Luke that Jed had to be around, someplace close by.

"Where's that damn Chance? Where is he?" asked Big Luke, as he crouched and began to nervously scan the creek bank and the surrounding trees.

"Well, Big Luke, I don't rightly know, but I 'spect he'll be showing up here just about any time."

"Reach down with your left hand, slow, real slow, and drop that gun belt, Mullins."

Craig unfastened his gun belt and tossed it onto the bank.

"Move, Craig, move past me and down the stream! I'm taking you back to camp then me and the boys will come back for Cap'n Chance, the bastard." And then, almost as an afterthought, "And where's Little Luke and Randy? They was back trailing — they — damn, just get moving, move or I'll drop you right here!"

The two men moved off in the fading light.

Chapter 16

Several hours earlier in the day, Sam Rogers, with two of his gang, rode into Lampasas. They headed for Jerry Scott's Saloon. In the past, Mart Horrell had told Sam that he usually could be found there, or a message could be left for him with the bartender, Eustis Wicker.

The three outlaws entered the saloon and found it nearly empty except for three ranch hands playing poker in one corner while two sporting gals looked on.

The three outlaws went to the bar where a man was wiping the bar down with a well-used bar rag.

Sam said, "Hey friend, how 'bout pouring my two friends some whiskey and get me a beer. We're looking for a fella name of Eustis, Eustis Wicker."

"Sure bud, that'll be me. What can I do for ya?" responded Wicker, as he moved to fill glasses, and grab the beer and placed them in front of the three men.

"Well, yeah, I need some information on a friend of mine, Mart Howell. You know where I might catch up to 'em?" asked Sam.

Leaning over the bar, and in low tones, Wicker said, "Well, friend, I knowed exactly who you be speaking on, but I wouldn't go dropping that name to just any old body in this town. Right now, ole Mart and his brothers ain't too popular with the town folk."

"Well, what's got them riled up on 'em?"

"Back in January Mart and his brothers killed ole Shad Denson, our sheriff and in March Mart and 'em killed four State Police officers, right here in this here saloon. They got put in jail but busted out and now they is on the run. Jerry, the owner of this place, is on the run with 'em. I heard tell they was headed for the New Mexico territory, maybe Lincoln County, but don't know for sure."

Sam sipped his beer as he mulled over what he had been told. Meanwhile, Rio and Jim had struck up a conversation with the two saloon girls and had just finished up the negotiation process and were headed for the upstairs rooms.

"God damned!" muttered Sam. "Just damn it all to hell, ain't nothing seeming to work out!"

Hearing his boss cussing, Rio stopped, "Everything ok, Sam?

"No, not by a damn site, but you boys tend to what you got. I'm going to find something to eat and a soft bed. We'll be headed out of this berg in the morning first thing after breakfast and getting some supplies so don't be late."

"Sure thing, Sam, we gon'a be a might lighter, though!" said Rio and both outlaws laughed as they followed the women upstairs.

Sam turned to leave and tossed a twenty-dollar gold piece on the bar, "Much obliged for the drinks and info and how 'bout taking a bottle up to my friends. If'n you do hear from Mart, tell him Sam Rogers was asking on 'em. I'd like to hook up with 'em sometime soon."

"Hold on there," replied Wicker, as he looked around to see if the poker playing cowboys were watching. "You might want to be taking that yeller 'kerchief off and tucking it away for a bit. Seems that a week or so ago there came in a telegraph 'bout a bank robbery in Dallas, two girls missing, and the leader was wearing a yeller—"

"Hey, thanks, thanks a lot. I'll be owing you one. You got new law here?"

"Well, just the state police right now, but they knowed 'bout the robbery, I guess, 'pert sure anyways."

"Thanks again." replied Sam, as he left the bar in search of a good steak while stuffing his yellow kerchief into his back pocket. His plan had been to hook up with Mart Horrell and his brothers and spend a few days resting up in Lampasas but being that the Horrell gang was on the run, he was going to have to change plans. Instead of going back to camp in the morning, he would give Rio and Jim Turner a couple of hours to take the edge off, then send one of them back to camp to get the boys headed this way pronto. He'd have to think on what to do with that girl. He could give the rest of his men tomorrow to taste the town then light out first thing the next morning for New Mexico. He would head for Lincoln County and hope to catch up with the Horrells there.

Chapter 17

Jed was bending over the low fire, pouring himself some coffee when he heard the horses moving through the brush.

"Dang boy, you gon'a let 'em drink up the whole creek," He was saying as he looked up, expecting to see Craig leading the horses into camp. Only it was just the horses. His big black followed by Craig's buckskin, both with reins trailing the ground.

With instincts born of living a life of trouble and danger, Jed immediately knew something was wrong. He dropped his cup and kicked dirt over the small fire and quickly taking up the horses' reigns he moved them under the trees and hobbled them.

He snatched up his coach gun and moved toward the creek, trying, in the fading light, to follow the horses trail. Moving as fast as the dared he reached the creek where Craig had been watering the horses. Jed bent down and striking a match off the butt of his .45, he scanned the ground for tracks. He saw two sets. One he recognized as Craig's. The other set of tracks he did not recognize but knew they didn't bode well for his friend. That was confirmed when moving the match around a bit he found Craig's gun belt lying in the mud. He could just make out the tracks headed up the creek, Craig in front and the other man trailing him. Without hesitation, he picked up Craig's gun belt and began moving up the creek, staying low and trying to move as quiet as possible but also with haste. If it was Sam Rogers and his boys that had taken Craig, he wouldn't last long and then the outlaws would come looking for him.

In the outlaw camp, the men were finishing up supper and Bob Rogers was just coming into camp, pulling up his pants, buckling his gun belt on and saying, "Damnit, we got to get some decent food 'sides these here Pecos Strawberries we down to eat'n. They is tearing my ass up!"

"Hello, the camp! I am coming in with a 'pert nice surprise for you boys!"

Entering through the bushes into camp was Big Luke McCoy with Craig Mullins at the end of his gun barrel.

"Well, I'll be damned!" blurted Bob, "Just look

at what Big Luke done caught down at that creek! Hey boys, check him out! You remember old Craig here from us paying a visit to him at his wore out old ranch outside of Dallas. Sam says he's the one done shot our friend, Jeff and kilt him for sure."

Spanish Bob, Bill Franks and Jess Fuller, the other men in camp, began hooting and yelling and moving toward Big Luke and Craig.

"We'll just have to return the favor in kind then won't we!" shouted Spanish Bob.

"Yea, let's give 'em some of the same medicine he done give Jeff!" yelled Jess Fuller.

The men had gathered around Craig and were punching his back, sides, and belly as they talked, just warming to their task. Then they began beating him in earnest.

All the commotion in camp woke Katherine Henderson from her fitful sleep. The outlaws had tied her hands and feet and laid her beside a log where she huddled under a thin blanket and tried not to think about her sister's fate and what was going to happen to her.

Katherine struggled to a sitting position and, looking over the log she laid against, she saw the outlaws beating up a dark-haired man who had fallen to his knees in the middle of the group. Fear for this man caused her to let out a scream which stopped the beating and caused the outlaws to look in her direction. The man on the ground looked at Katherine and said through clenched teeth and bloody lips, "Your grandma sent me and my friend to fetch you home. He will be along shortly, he's a big man and blonde, you do what he says when he comes, and you'll be fine. He — "

Bob kicked Craig in the side ending his musing to Katherine and causing Craig to retch.

"Yea, 'bout that partner of yours, boy, where might he be?" Then glaring at Katherine, "and you, girl, you best shut up or I'm gon'a hide you 'til breakfast!"

"I found old Craig here watering horses a ways up the creek. I didn't see nobody else and didn't want to run into Cap'n Chance if he was about, so I scurried on back to camp with this 'un," said Big Luke, as he motioned toward Craig.

At the mention of Chance, Bob remembered, and turning to Jess Fuller and Bill Franks said, "You two, move into those trees yonder, get out to 'bout the edge of this grove and 'bout twenty yards apart and keeps 'a watch for anything moving to our camp."

"You want Bill and me to just go on up to their camp and take care of this Chance fella?" asked Jess.

Bob and Big Luke exchanged glances then Bob said, "No, 'cause I want that you two live long enough to see tomorrow! So, do what I told ya!"

As the two outlaws picked up their rifles and headed to sentry duty, Big Luke spoke quietly to the two men," You boys be watchful, more watchful than any time in your life. This man, Chance, we seen what he can do. He's... he's death come to flesh."

The two men just stared at Big Luke and with a nod and grin moved off into the brush.

"Now," said Spanish Bob, as he moved to Craig and grabbed him under the arms and lifted his, "let's tie this ole Craig to a tree and have a little fun!"

"Yea, well, 'fore we have fun I want to know where my brother is," said Big Luke.

"Yep, Randy too," said Bob Rogers.

As the three men drug Craig to a tree and began tying him to it, Katherine Henderson lay curled up and praying that the man was right, and someone was going to save her and take her home. She prayed hard on it.

Some time earlier, in Lampasas, Jim Turner reluctantly mounted his horse and headed back to the outlaw camp. Sam had come to the room where Jim was sporting with one of the whores from the saloon and told him to get to camp and hustle back with the men and he would keep Jim's whore warm for him until he returned. It pissed Jim off, but a man didn't argue with Sam, you just did what you're told. Sam had also told him that they couldn't risk bringing the girl to town, so they could use her up then kill her. Jim knew he wasn't going to do the deed, but he knew none of the others would have a problem doing for her, after they had a little fun with her, of course. He was going to hurry, least ways, as much as the dark would allow.

Chapter 18

Jed was moving quietly but as fast as possible down the stream. As he moved around a bend in the creek, he heard, before he saw, the horses in the water. Moving slowly up to the horses so he wouldn't startle them, he could see there were six of them with reigns trailing in the water so he figured there were at least six men in the outlaw camp. Standing still and slowing his breathing he closed his eyes and listened while testing the air for odors. There, the sound of men laughing and the smell of a campfire! Jed moved to the bank and slipped off his boots and left them on the bank with Craig's rig. He checked that his handguns were loose in their holsters, took up his coach gun and then quietly moved off in the direction of the sounds he had heard. He moved slowly, sliding his bare feet along the ground, testing for branches, twigs, or rocks. He used his bare feet or knelt and used his hand to move things that would give him away if he stepped on them. His breathing was controlled. He moved without a sound. He pulled his bowie knife.

Jess Fuller was leaning with his back to a big pecan tree, looking to the north. He couldn't figure what the big deal was with this Chance character. He and Bill were plenty capable enough to roust him out and finish him off. His back itched and he rubbed it against the tree as he was thinking about finding Bill and going after this supposed great fighter when an arm suddenly snaked around his neck and he was pulled back against what at first felt like a large boulder. He couldn't breathe and his attempts to remove the arm from around his neck were futile.

"You alone out here?" asked the soft whisper in his ear.

"Uggg, ugg, Can't sp—"

Another whisper, "You part of the bunch what took those girls?"

"Ugggggh! Sam—Sam took—!"

Keeping his powerful arm locked around the struggling man's throat, "Yea, you is one of them and you ain't alone. Somebody done rolled one to smoke, 'bout due east of here, I reckon. Stupid," whispered Jed in the struggling man's ear.

"Uggg, can't brea—!"

"I know. Troublesome, ain't it. I'll fix that for 'ya."

Jess Fuller felt the bowie knife bite deep on the left side of his neck. He felt the blood spurt and felt a horrible pain as the big knife was pulled slowly and effortlessly across his neck, sliding through, opening him up and—

Jed laid the lifeless body on the ground and moved on, seeking out the other sentry, the one smoking, the stupid one.

Back in camp, the outlaws had finished tying Craig to the tree. The three men had resumed taking turns beating Craig. Craig knew he has some broken ribs and busted lips and had lost one tooth and several more that his probing tongue had found were loose. He figured that by this time Jed would have discovered he was missing and would be looking for him. He hoped he would find him in time.

And for the tenth time from Big Luke, "Dam it, Craig! Tell me what happened to my brother or I swear I'm—!"

"I kil— I kilt him —you—damn fool. Kilt him, Randy too. I kilt both of 'em!"

"Well, then, you fuck'n bastard, I'm gon'a open you up and see what you got inside!" yelled Big Luke McCoy, as he pulled his knife and started toward the tied man.

"Hold on Luke! Hold on! You can carve him some, but don't kill him. We got to wait for Sam 'fore we go killing Mr. Mullins," said Bob Rogers.

"'Shore, 'shore, I won't kill him none. Just carve a bit."

Bob and Spanish Bob laughed as Big Luke's backhand swipe with his knife cut Craig from left hip to his right nipple. Craig screamed.

It was a natural clearing in the woods. Nature made, not man. Jed silently stepped through the brush at the northern most side of the clearing just as Big Luke's knife was cutting Craig's chest. He had heard the men laughing and talking about not killing his friend, just carving him a bit. The clearing was some sixty feet across from where Jed stood to where the men had Craig tied. The night was full on dark; the forest was silent except for a little breeze just moving the uppermost branches of the tall oaks and pecan trees. Jed took it all in. To his left, he saw the girl. He was shocked she was still alive. The crackling fire, the men's laughter, and the soft sobs of the woman and Craig's moans were the only noises to be heard.

Some fifteen or so feet to Jed's left and with her back against an old fallen tree, Katherine lay curled up, eyes closed, tears streaming as she silently prayed for the man to come and save her and prayed for the man being hurt. Her body trembled and shook when she heard the man scream. Before the echo of his scream had died, and with the bad men still laughing, she felt someone close. She opened her eyes and stared at a pair of bare feet. She looked up— and up, and looked into the kindest pair of blue eyes she had ever seen.

The tall man knelt, put his lips to her ear and whispered, "I've come for you, Katherine. I am gon'a take you home. Now, just lay here and give me a minute and I will be back for you. I promise."

The man's big hand stroked her hair, he smiled and used his fingers to gently close her eyes and was gone.

Chapter 19

Jed stepped over the log that Katherine was sheltered behind and soundlessly moved toward the men torturing Craig. The world slowed down for Jed. The men in front of him seemed to move so slowly and everything stood out in stark and vivid colors and shapes. As he moved towards them his eyes missed nothing.

It was full dark, but the outlaws had thrown several big logs on the fire in the middle of the clearing and the logs were blazing. Nothing else in the forest made a sound. It was as if the night creatures knew that danger was in their midst, so all had sought distance from this spot.

"Go on Big Luke! Give 'em another swipe with that pig sticker. Open 'em up a bit more!" shouted Spanish Bob.

Big Luke was preparing to do just that when—

The sound of the hammers being eared back on Jed's 10-gauge coach gun was audible to all in the clearing.

The three outlaws turned as one each reaching for their sidearms but each froze when they saw Jed with the shotgun pointing at them.

Big Luke and Bob Rogers knew Jed, but Spanish Bob had never made his acquaintance. The figure of Jed Chance in the firelight was a frightful one and sent a shiver of fear through Bob. He saw a giant of a man, six feet four and well over two hundred pounds and all muscle, long blonde hair cascading to his powerful shoulders; a blonde, drooping mustache adorned his face along with a vicious scar that seemed to stand out in the flickering light. The blood of the two dead sentries tracked over his vest and shirt sleeve. The fact that he stood there in his bare feet just seemed to add to the primitive danger of this man. In his left hand, Chance held his shotgun and his right hung loose and relaxed next to his holstered iron. The big man's eyes! Even at the distance of twenty or so feet, Spanish Bob could see that were bright blue and in them danced rage, and — Death!

The outlaws were each rendered speechless and Jed could see that Bob Rogers was looking over his shoulder as if expecting someone to come up behind him.

"They won't be joining us, Bob. Those boys you sent out to keep watch. I did for 'em."

Raising his head, Craig said, "'bout time you got here, Jed. I was giving 'em all they wanted and was 'bout to—"

"Yea, Pard, I see that I got here just in time to save these here boys from the whipping you was 'bout to lay on 'em. Now, Big Luke, take that knife of your's and cut Craig down from that tree, and ease him down slow like, so I know you ain't got no ill intention on my friend."

After a moment of hesitation, Big Luke turned and cut Craig down and eased him to the ground then turned to face Jed.

Spanish Bob was to Jed's left and Bob Rogers and Big Luke a little to his right. Jed stood relaxed and loose, waiting for one of the men to make a move. There was no doubt in any of the men in that clearing that no quarter would be given, and none would be asked.

Bob Rogers had recovered his senses and after assessing the situation figured that the odds were in their favor. He said, "Ok Jed, you got the drop on us but now what 'ca gon'a do? There are three of us agin just you. I say you drop that shotgun and get shed of your pistols and we'll all just wait here for Sam to get back. The fact is you and old Craig there can share that tree. So, boy, by the time I count to —"

"Shut up, Bob, just shut your mouth! Damn, you always was the mouthy one of you boys. Least ways Randy didn't get all mouth 'fore I killed 'em."

"You killed Randy? Craig said he —"

"Yea, I heard him taking credit for that. I killed him and Little Luke, a few miles north of that grove where you boys killed Rose Henderson. Killed Little Luke fast but gut shot old Randy so's it would take him time to die. I left him on a little rise, bleeding out. Hopefully, the wolves or something got to him 'fore he passed on."

Craig heard this and raised his head, "Thought you said he was dead?"

"Yea, Pard, I lied some 'bout that. I didn't want you to fret on it."

During this conversation, Jed had lowered his shotgun so now it was pointing more at the ground than the outlaws. This wasn't lost on the three outlaws and Spanish Bob, taking his lead from the bravado of Bob Rogers said, "Yea, we finished that other girl, but not 'fore we all got some of that blonde bitch." Then grasping his crotch with his left hand while his right hand flashed for his iron, he shouted, "And I gave her all of this here!"

The roar of the shotgun filled the forest! Jed, with a flick of his wrist, fired both barrels of the coach gun into Spanish Bob's crotch and eighteen pieces of buckshot removed Spanish Bob's left hand and everything below his navel that would have identified him as a man. His body was thrown back ten feet into the brush. In that same instant both Bob Rogers and Big Luke pulled iron and Jed's right hand was a blur of movement as his colt cleared leather and his left hand, now empty of the shotgun, came over in a flash. As Jed spun to his right in a crouch he fanned three quick rounds that were so close together they were as one roar. Big Luke had just cleared leather when Jed's first round plowed the soft tissue under his chin and out the top of his head. He was dead before he hit the ground. Bob Rogers cleared leather and got off a shot, but it just plowed dirt at his feet as two rounds entered Bob's chest and must have hit some solid things because they never came out the back side of him. He dropped to the ground next to Craig, dead.

With the sound of gunfire filling the camp, Katherine screamed.

Jed holstered his .45 and moved toward her while yelling at Craig over his shoulder, "Let me see to the girl, I 'll be back with 'ya in a minute or two!"

"Go ahead, boy, I'll just sit here with ole Bob and bleed!" Craig yelled back.

Jed hustled to Katherine and kneeling he pulled his knife and cut the ropes binding her hands and feet and pulled her to him.

"Shhhh, don't cry. Please don't cry. You're free. I'm gon'a to take you home; me and Craig are gon'a take you home."

Katherine struggled to choke back her sobs and gain control of her emotions and for the first time she got a good look at her savior's face. She saw a big man, his clothes were dirty, his hair was dirty, he was bare-foot, and his face was grimy with flecks of blood on his cheeks and he had a big scar on his face. His shirt sleeve and vest had lots of blood spots all over them. She looked into his blue eyes. He smiled at her. He was the most handsome man she had ever seen.

Easily picking Katherine up in his arms, "Now, I'm gon'a sit you over by the fire and give you a canteen of water to sip on while I see to old Craig over yonder.

He's got a cut or two that need fixing."

"The men beat him up. I heard them, but he told me you were coming and that you would save me, but Rose is dead, she's dead, I know it!"

Sitting Katherine down by the fire facing away from the carnage he had wrought, Jed handed her one of the outlaw's canteen.

"Yea, Rose is dead. We found her, and Craig and I saw to burying her. I'm sorry for her and you and your Grandma, but I did for them that harmed her and you, least ways, nearly all."

The rebel yell pierced the night as Jim Turner came charging into camp shoving reins in his teeth and pulling a gun in each hand, he commenced to blazing away at Jed! Jed grabbed Katherine as she let out a scream, and, turning his back to the charging man, he dove to the ground, covering her body with his. His right hand struggled to find his .45 but Katherine's kicking leg knocked his hand away! Turner's first shot hit in the fire, showering Jed and Katherine with sparks, his second kicked dirt in Jed 's eyes and his third plowed a white-hot furrow across Jed 's shoulder. Jed tensed for the next shot when, from his left, a shot rang out, then two more in quick succession. There never was another shot from Jim Turner. His lifeless body flew from his horse and hit the ground. One round had found his chest; another had torn open his throat.

Jed looked to his left and there was Craig, leaning against the tree he had been tied to, and with the late Bob Roger's Colt 1860, still smoking, in his hand.

Jed stared.

"Yea, I know, I need to work on my speed."

"Well, you did let 'em get off three shots, one of which—"

"Damn Jed! I ought to—"

"No, no, not in front of the girl."

Both men smiled, even Katherine smiled.

"Get me up and out o' here, Jed, 'fore more of them boys show up."

"Yep, let's move. Get back to our camp and head for town. You need doctoring and I think I need seeing after and Katherine here too."

Craig watched as Jed tended to Katherine and got her ready to travel. He watched his friend and then began to feel a weight in his hand. He looked down at the still smoking Colt and the reality of what had just happened began to register on him. He had saved his friend and the girl and did what he did without hesitation but now the fact there was more blood on his hands weighed on him, another death to deal with. His hand began to shake, and his stomach knotted and he tossed the gun aside like it was burning his hand — or his soul.

Jed left Katherine with Craig and returned to the stream where he retrieved his boots and Craig's rig and gathering up the reins of the outlaw's horses took them back to camp. They mounted two of the horses with Katherine riding with Jed, her arms wrapped tightly around his waist and headed back to their own camp. The dead lay where they had fallen.

Chapter 20

Sam Rogers woke with a bad headache and the taste of bad whiskey in his mouth and the whore he had spent the night with snoring in his ear. He had drunk more of the saloon's whiskey than he intended and was paying for it now. Drawing both legs up to his stomach, he put both feet in the stomach of the snoring whore and gave a might push! The woman hit the floor with an ugly noise and a tangle of feet, legs, arms and bed clothes.

"Hey — what the — what you — !"

"Shut up and go get me some coffee, and do it now!"

The woman rubbed her ass with one hand while she struggled to her feet.

"Well, 'ya didn't have — "

"Not another word, woman! Get my coffee, and stop by my friend's room and make sure he's awake. Tell him to meet me at the bar in thirty minutes. Now, hurry up!"

The woman left to get the coffee all the while cursing and muttering under her breath and wishing all kinds of vile things upon the head of the outlaw.

Sam got up and. scratching at his crotch and stretching, he looked out the window of the room to the street below. He reckoned it was about seven o'clock or just before. Jim should have been back into town with Bob and the rest of the men hours ago. Sam figured they were laid up at the corral or elsewhere in the saloon.

Sam was dressed when the woman returned with his coffee and he had barely taken a sip when Rio came running into the room.

"We got trouble, Sam! Get on downstairs, now, 'cause we got big trouble!"

Rio wasn't the sort to be yelling "wolf" unless there was trouble. Sam didn't say a word, just grabbed up his gun belt and hat as he followed Rio out of the room and down the stairs.

As soon as the two men approached the bar, Sam could tell something was up. Two dozen or so of the town's citizens were there, some standing, some sitting and all talking at once. Something had them riled up.

Wicker was back behind the bar and Sam could

see by the man's wide-eyed and frightened expression that something was indeed up.

Sliding up to the bar and looking as calm as possible Sam spoke to Wicker and Rio, who was standing at his side, "Boys, whatever is happening, let's try not to look like we got any concern at all, nope, not nary a one. Now, Rio, I don't see no law in here and no one woke me up with a gun in my face so stay calm and watch the front door and, Eustis, why don't you get a smile on that face, pour us some of that coffee there, and tell me, calm like, what the hell is going on."

Picking up two cups and the pot of coffee and pouring, Eustis said, "Early morning, 'fore light, two men, and a girl come riding in. One man was beat up and cut up; ta'other was hurt a little too. The girl was a frightful mess but ok, I guess. It was one of them girls that got taken from Dallas! Those two men took her from the outlaw's camp, somewhere outside of town. They…"

Sam's fear and anger had risen with each word Eustis spoke.

"Well, spit it out! What the fuck—"

"They're dead, all dead in the camp—camp of the outlaws. The one man kilt them all, I think."

Sam looked down at the coffee in front of him and, in a whisper, "All dead? All of em?"

"Yea, that's what one of the State Police guys, that was in here earlier, said."

"What did these two hombres look like, Eustis?"

"Well, I ain't laid eyes on 'em but was told that the one of 'em, the one that did the killing is — "

"He's big, he's big and blonde," interrupted Sam.

"Well, yeah, that's what they say. You know 'em?"

"Yea, I know 'em. Name is Jed, Jed Chance. Mind you remember that name, Eustis. His partner, the other man he came in with, is Craig Mullins."

All during the conversation Sam's eyes never stopped staring into his coffee and his knuckles were white from his squeezing the cup hard, so hard that the cup shook.

Rio eased back a step. He never took his eyes off the front door, but he knew what Sam could be like when riled up and he could tell that his boss was really riled. Wicker took a step back also and nervously twisted a bar rag in his hands.

Finally, Sam looked up and, though his eyes shone wetly, he spoke calmly to both men, "Rio, go get our horses. Take your time, pay the stable hand and meet me back here when you're done. Nobody's gon'a recognize you here. You were masked at the bank and Jed and Craig don't know you. Just in case, though, keep your hat low and don't look nobody square in the face. Go."

Rio moved off through the crowd to get the horses as Sam ordered.

"Now, Eustis, where might these two men be now?"

"Said they was at Doctor Denny's office, Thomas Denny, he's a new doc in town, been here 'bout a year or so."

"Well, you get me a mess of eggs and biscuits and then draw me a map of where this Pill's office is. I need to pay him and his patients a visit."

Wicker moved off to get Sam's food and a map. Sam went back to staring into his coffee. He was seeing two brothers lost. His eyes were wet again.

Chapter 21

Jed, Craig and Katherine had arrived in Lampasas in the very early morning hours. They had made it to a livery stable where Jed told the watchman there to get a doctor and any law available in town. They had been taken to the doctor's office where they spent several hours getting Craig stitched and patched up, Jed's shoulder tended, and Katherine cleaned up. There was a woman who showed up to help the doctor. Jed pulled her aside and after a quiet conversation between the two, she took Katherine upstairs. After about thirty minutes they came back down with Katherine looking a little embarrassed, but the lady gave Jed a slight smile and whispered to him that Katherine was indeed fine except for the bruises and lack of food. The livery watchman brought two state police officers to the doctor's office and Jed told them all that had happened since he and Craig had departed Dallas.

When Jed related what had happened that night

with the outlaws the two policemen looked at each other and then back at Jed. The younger of the two said, "Now, hold on mister. You say you walked into their camp and bested three, no five outlaws? I don't think that is—"

"It's like he said," said Craig from where he lay on the doctor's table. "Every word he said is the truth. He killed them all, his own self. Well, 'cept for one I dropped. I had to cover Jed's back."

The two friends looked at each other and smiled.

"Well," said the younger of the two policemen, "We'll just send out some men to check all this out. Then we'll—"

The older officer had been eyeing Jed closely. The lawman had the look of rawhide tough and many tough miles traveled and eyes that didn't miss much. He interrupted the other officer.

"Mr. Chance—"

"Jed."

"Well, Jed, seems like you most likely are the Jed Chance that marshaled down south Texas way a few years back. Least ways, you got the look of that man."

"Yea, that'll be me, for sure."

"Ummm, well, ok then. Way I hear it 'bout you,

you most likely could do what you said you did."

The younger policeman spoke up again, "We'll send some men out at first light and bring in the bodies and horses. Then—"

"You go out and get their horses, their personals and such and check for any of them having any of that stolen bank money on 'em, but you leave them bodies where they lay. Them boys chose their dying ground. You let 'em lay where they are. There's no burying for 'em." Jed had spoken low but no one in the room doubted that there would be hell to pay if his instructions weren't followed.

"Now, see here, Mr. Chance, we—" started the younger officer but his partner placed his hand gently on the young man's arm and said, "We'll handle it, Mr. Chance—Jed. We'll do as you ask."

"Thanks," said Jed. "Now, can one of you direct me to a telegraph office? I want to send a message to Sheriff Barkley in Dallas and let him know what's going on."

"Sure, Jed, I'll take you over. Brodie, you stay here. I'll be back shortly," said the older officer to his friend. With that, he headed for the door with Jed close behind.

Sheriff Barkley was standing outside his office having just finished his morning coffee when Paul Gibbs, the telegraph operator, came running up.

"Sheriff, Sheriff! It's a message from that Chance fella!" Gibbs was holding the message up and waving it in the air. Breathless, he bent over to regain his composure and breath as he handed the message to Sheriff Barkley who tore open the message and read;

Katherine safe. Stop. Most outlaws dead. Stop. Craig hurt some. stop. Will hold up in Lampasas two days then to Dallas. Stop. Advise Mrs. Henderson and Ruth.

JC

The Sheriff re-read the message twice, and then it hit him. There was no mention of Rose. He knew what that must mean. With a mixture of joy and sadness he headed over to the hotel where Mrs. Henderson had been staying since the two rescuers had left town. He was not looking forward to telling her the news about Rose.

After sending the message to Sheriff Barkley, Jed headed back to the Doctor's office with the policeman, whose name he learned was David Riley. Halfway back they were stopped by a messenger sent by the policeman, Brodie. The doctor had moved Craig and Katherine to the hotel where they would be more comfortable and could get proper rest. The two men altered their course and headed for the hotel.

Across from the doctor's office, in a narrow alley, Sam Rogers, and Rio crouched, each armed with a Yellow Boy 44-40. They were waiting for Jed and Craig to come out of the doctor's office. They would ambush and kill the two men right here and anyone else who got in their way.

They had been waiting some time when they saw a man with a doctor's bag coming down the street and enter the office.

"What the hell, Sam? Shouldn't that old sawbones have been in there fixing whatever those boys needed fixing? I don't think them boys is there anymore," said Rio.

"Sure seems like that. Tell ya what. They don't know you, so slip over there and see what you can find out. Tell that doc you're a just curious 'bout them boys. See what you can find out."

Rio hustled over to the doctor's office and let

himself in. In ten or so minutes he came out of the office and headed over to where Sam waited in the shadows, "Well, seems like that Mullins fellow was hurt some and needed some sewing and doctoring and some for Chance too. They got the girl all right. They been put up at the hotel and the law is headed out to the camp to collect things. Sam, that doc looked at me real hard like. I think he was real suspicious. He—"

Movement from across the street drew their attention and they saw the doctor leaving his office and hurrying up the street while looking over his shoulder.

"We got to move, Sam. Things are getting hot here."

"Let's go to that hotel first. Maybe we will get a shot at those bastards 'fore we high-tail it out of here."

The two outlaws moved calmly to the hotel. Taking up positions across the street, they observed four state policemen at the entrance in conversation with several of the town's citizens. Other townspeople huddled in various small groups in front of the hotel discussing the exciting news of outlaws, kidnapping, and death.

Sam turned to Rio and handed him his rifle and told him he was going over to the hotel and see what he could learn.

"This is damn chancey, Sam. We need to get out 'a this town muy pronto!"

"I know, Rio, but I gots to find out what happened and kill those two sons of bitches!"

"Ok, Sam. I'll cover you from here. If'n things go south, head for the horses and I'll meet you there."

"Right."

With that, Sam moved across the street and, rolling a smoke, eased up on the hotel porch and approached one of the policemen.

"Hey friend, you got a light on 'ya?"

"Yea, think I got one here," replied the officer as he searched his vest pockets for a match. Finding one, he lit it with his thumb and then held it while Sam got his smoke going.

"Lots of excitement in town; I heard that some outlaws got killed. That right?"

"Yea, they are dead as yesterday. Big blonde fella name of Chance and his friend did 'em. They was the outlaws that robbed that Dallas bank and took them girls. One of them girls is dead, the other's gon'a be ok. We went to their camp and sure enough, there was six dead outlaws. Six! They was shot, some cut. That man kilt them boys three ways to Sunday, he did. No bury'n 'em either. Chance said not to and Riley, our Captain, said let it be. He don't want no trouble with Chance but I 'spect when they leave town in a day or two, then we'll slip out and bury 'em — or maybe not."

"So, they got 'em all then."

"Nope, don't think so. Chance and his friend are upstairs now giving Cap'n Riley a description of the leader of the gang. He weren't in their camp and Chance thinks he's in Lampasas or close by. We get that description; we'll track him down, for sure. We catch 'em — we — we — "

Turning to one of his fellow officers the policeman said, "Hey Brodie — Brodie! Look yonder." The officer pointed across the street where moments before Rio had been leaning against a store front.

"What is it? "Brodie asked.

"Well, he's done gone now but there was a fellow over to the store there and he was all in black and had a Concho gun belt on just like doc said that fellow what visited his office and asked a bunch of questions was wearing. He's disappeared awful fast."

"Come on, let's see if we can round this hombre up," said Brodie.

The two policemen hurried across the street in

search of the man with the Concho gun belt and Sam took his leave and headed to where he and Rio had left their horses.

When Sam arrived, Rio was already mounted and waiting. Sam threw himself into his saddle and turning his horse to head west and out of town he said to Rio, "The law is on to you and soon as Chance and Mullins get through telling 'em 'bout me, they'll be on to me too! It won't be today, but I'll get those sons of bitches! I'll see 'em both in the dirt and bleeding out if it's the last thing—"

"Let it go, for now, Sam. We'll get to New Mexico, then get back here in a few months with the Horrell boys and kill 'em both, slow like."

"Yep, that's what will do, slow death for them bastards!" said Sam. Reaching into his back-pocket Sam pulled out his yellow kerchief and tied it around his neck. "Now, let's ride!"

Chapter 22

They had been in Lampasas for three rainy days recuperating from their wounds and Jed was eager to get started back to Dallas and reunite Katherine with her grandmother. The morning had come to them with dark clouds and the promise of more rain. He and Craig were in the hotel packing while in her room Katherine was being visited by two women from the town. Different women had come each day to stay with her and offer support and sympathy, but everyone could tell she wasn't comfortable and at ease unless she was with Jed. She stayed with him as much as possible and insisted he take every meal with her and she rarely would leave her room unless he accompanied her.

They had visited a local store and gotten Katherine new clothes for traveling. She loved the clothes but only really embraced them when she saw how Jed looked at her and smiled when she tried them on. Katherine was tall for a woman, but she had to get on her tiptoes to give Jed a big kiss on the cheek as thanks for the outfit. Craig knew the ways of women much better than Jed and he told his big friend that it appeared to him that Katherine was smitten with him, or, at least, he thought she was. Jed laughed at Craig and said it was just gratefulness for them saving her that made her act the way she did, and just fear of being alone.

The two friends were in their room packing when there was a knock on the door. Craig opened it and Captain Riley stepped into the room.

"You boys 'bout ready to head out?" he asked.

"Yep, just 'bout," said Jed. "We figured on getting a start this morning early 'fore the rain sets in again, but, well, what with waiting on a woman and all, we—"

"You don't got to explain that to me, Jed. I got a wife and two daughters, so I know, believe me, I know. Look here Jed, we been passing that description around on that outlaw leader, Sam Rogers, and we might have stumbled on something."

Jed turned to face Riley as he buckled his gun belt on, "Oh yeah, well good. What you got?"

"A couple of punchers that hang out over at Jerry Scott's saloon said they saw these two hombres in conversation with Eustis Wicker, the bartender there, and one of them swears one was dressed all in black and he called the other fella, 'Sam'. I'm going over there now to brace Wicker and wanted to know if you wanted to come along?"

"Hell yea, I'm with 'ya. Craig, get Katherine to hurry along and I'll meet you two in front of the hotel. The liveryman brought our horses over and I got a horse for Katherine too. We got a pack horse with grub and stuff so we're ready to go when I finish at the bar. Well, depending on what this Wicker fellow says—anyway, meet me out front."

"Will do, but I still ain't moving so fast so take your time," said Craig as he gingerly pulled on his shit as Jed and Riley went out the door.

Craig finished getting dressed and leaving his room he stopped and rapped on Katherine's door. He called through the door that he was going downstairs for coffee and would wait for her there and that Jed was off with Riley and would be meeting them out front in a bit. He heard an ok from Katherine and headed down the stairs, taking care to protect his ribs.

He was sitting at a table sipping his second cup of coffee when Katherine came down the stairs. Some of the towns ladies and tried to dress her in a black mourning dress due to the death of Rose but she refused. She had told all that she would miss Rose every day of her life, but she wasn't going to mourn every day. This morning she was dressed in a white shirt, black riding pants, and a low brim, black hat that her ebony hair sprung from in every direction, except the front.

She arrived at Craig's table with her carry bag and sitting down requested from the waiter a cup of coffee and a biscuit. He was quick to oblige her.

Her morning fare arrived and taking a sip of the coffee, she asked, "So, where is Jed?"

Riley thinks he may have stumbled on Sam Rogers' trail, leastways they headed over to the saloon to check it out."

"Well, uh, I mean, do you think Jed will be all right, I mean, maybe we should—"

"Miss. Katherine, Jed Chance is the most all right fella you ever going to meet."

"Well, I wouldn't want someone to—"

"It would most likely take a lot more than a "someone", Katherine. It would take a heap of folks to bring Jed down. 'Sides, Riley looks like he can take care of his self too so they should be fine, them two."

"I just don't want anything to—"

"Get'n sweet on 'em, are ya?

"What? No, no nothing like that!" shot back a little embarrassed Katherine. "It's just that, well, he probably has a wife or a girlfriend somewhere and I just…

"Nope, don't, not neither. He had a wife, but he tells it that she died some years back from something. So, my friend has just me, my woman, Ruth, and boy Jeff. That's it."

"No mother or father, no siblings at all?"

"Uh—sib—wha—Oh, you mean brother or sister. No, none of that. I know you are curious, so I will tell 'ya but don't go talking on it too much with Jed. Jed's mom was a sporting lady in Atlanta. A man, some plantation owner, got her pregnant with Jed and another man beat her to death when Jed was just a boy. He's been on his own since. In a nutshell, that's Jed's story. 'Cepting of course, working barges on the Mississippi when still just a pup, the war and fighting and making Cap'n, and saving me and others a few dozen times, and being the best fight'n man I ever seen."

"Well, I thank you for the information about Jed," said Katherine as she shifted in her seat as if the conversation made her uncomfortable. Then, to fill the silence between them, "I know your, Ruth. She's a very

168

nice lady. She did some sewing on dresses that Rose... that Rose and I had shipped out from back east."

They sat in silence while they both finished their coffee and Craig began to roll a smoke.

"He seems like a good man."

Craig stopped in the midst of rolling and looked at the young girl. "Katherine, they ain't no man finer. No man more loyal or protective of his friends and no man better to ride the river with. He's a real good man, unless of course you get on his bad side, like them Rogers boys, then just make your peace 'cause you'll be dealing cards with the devil come soon."

Katherine stared at Craig, thinking on all he had said and what she had learned about Jed Chance. Putting down her cup and standing up to take up her bag she looked at Craig, who was peering at her through the smoke of his match as he put fire to his rolled smoke.

"I don't care. I don't care where he is from or where he has been. I like him. I like him a lot. He's — he's my friend."

Standing up, Craig adjusted his gun belt and looked at Katherine intently, "Good, he's a right good friend to have and, well, Katherine, if'n you had any other attitude on him, well, you and me couldn't be friends, so it's a good thing you see things as you do." Then taking Katherine by the elbow with one hand, taking her bag with the other and turning toward the door, "Now, let's you and me get on out to the horses 'cause he'll be along directly, I imagine."

Chapter 23

Eustis Wicker had just finished his breakfast and was sweeping the floor when Jed and Riley walked in. Eustis had been half way expecting a visit from Riley but he wasn't expecting the very big, scary looking blonde man coming in with the policeman. Wicker took one look at Jed and the look on his face and decided to step behind the bar to put something between himself and the man that had killed six or eight or ten outlaws, depending on who you talked to.

"Morning, Eustis."

"Morning, Riley. What can I do for 'ya,"

"Just some information on two hombres you were seen speaking to. You know the ones I mean. We been asking 'bout them all over town. There was one dressed in black and the other, name of 'Sam'. We hear tell that you spent some time parlaying with them two."

"Well, now, I ain't sure who you mean. I mean, I sees lots of folks—"

"Don't be shining me on, Eustis. I can see in your face you know who I'm speaking on! Now, you—"

"Hell with you law man! I don't got to tell—"

Jed had been standing behind and just to the right of Riley and like the policeman, he could tell in the shifty eyes of the bartender that he knew the men they were asking about. Before Wicker could finish his statement, Jed stepped around the policeman and grabbing the bartender by the shirt front with his left hand he effortlessly pulled the man over the bar and then roughly pushed him against it. It was too close to call as to who was more shocked, Riley or the bartender. At that moment, two townsmen wondered in and seeing what was happening just backed up against the door and stared.

"All right, barkeep, now hear me! I got no time for your lies and bullshit! Those men are bad men. They are robbers, rapist and killers of women! What did they want from you? What did you talk about with 'em?" asked Jed.

Feigning courage he did not feel, Wicker answered, "Now! You hold on. You got no right to grab me up! 'Sides, them boys are friends of the Horrell's so they be friends of mine. I ain't—"

Jed reached down and taking Wicker's right

hand in his left said, "Serving drinks just got harder, boy." Jed snapped the little finger on the hand and Wicker howled in shock and pain.

" Owwwwww! Shit, oh shit, man! What'd you — fuck! — fuck!"

Riley went to put his hand on Jed's arm but one look at the man's face made him hesitate.

Wicker was bent over in pain and holding his injured hand. Jed shoved Wicker upright and pulled the hand away and held it up in front of Wicker's face. The injured finger was bent back and almost touching the back of the man's hand. Wicker tried to pull away and in his pain and agony fell to his knees. Jed dropped to his knees but keeping the injured hand in front of the bartender's face. Shaking the hand, Jed said, "Now, boy, you got four more on this hand and five on the other and I surely will spend the rest of the day rearranging the appearance of each of them. Now, you tell me 'bout those men, Sam Rogers, and the other fellow or I'm gon'a do another!"

"Ok! Ok! Don't — not — no — They was looking for Mart Horrell and his bunch — told 'em Mart was gone to — to New Mexico — Lincoln County. They're headed there, sure of it as can be. They high tailed it out 'a town the morning you rode in." Looking up at Riley and pleading, "I need the doc, need 'em now!"

"I know Sam Rogers, but the man in black, what's his name?" asked Jed.

"Rio, Rio is all I know. Damn I'm hurt'n, hurt'n bad!"

Jed stood and looked down at the man and said, "I find out you have lied to me, I will be back and I will finish what I started." With that, he turned and headed for the door. Riley followed close behind and when they reached the door where the two townsmen stood in shock at what they had witnessed.

"So, you boys see what happened here?" asked the lawman.

"No, Cap'n Riley, we were just leaving and 'sides we don't hold with raping and killing women. So, no, we didn't see nothing 'cepting Wicker there slamming his finger in the bar door. Looks like he may have broke something too," replied one of the men while the other nodded his head in agreement.

"Yep, the way I saw it too. How 'bout letting the doc know to stop in here. Now, please excuse Mr. Chance and me, we have to be going," said Riley.

The two men left the bar and headed for the hotel.

Chance walked in silence but upon arriving at the hotel where Craig and Katherine, upon seeing him approaching, had mounted, he took the reins of his big mare in his hands and turned to the policeman and said, "Riley, sorry 'bout that situation with the barkeep. I know I overstepped but—"

"Don't rightly know what you mean, Chance, it was just a man getting his finger where it didn't belong." And taking Jed's big hand in his and shaking it, "You all have a safe trip back to Dallas. If'n I see or hear tell of that Rogers fella, I'll send word to Sheriff Barkley, but I figure that outlaw is half way to the New Mexico territory by now and none of us will hear from him ever again."

Thunder rolled in the distance and Jed pulled a slicker from the pack horse put it on and mounted his big mare.

Chance said, "Don't bet on that Riley. This ain't over, not for Mrs. Henderson, and since I killed his brothers, not for Sam Rogers, and sure as hell not for me. Not by a long shot. Might be that you go ahead and send a message to Barkley and let him know we're headed that way. We should make Dallas in seven or eight days depending on how Katherine travels. He don't see us in eight, he better come look'n and damn quick. And Riley, keep an eye on that bar keep. If there comes something you think I need to know, how about sending a telegram to Dallas. The sheriff will get it to me."

"I'll do my best, Jed, but the state police ain't gon'a be around much longer. The new governor, Coke, I hear is bringing back the rangers. Folks in Texas don't like us much no way. Time comes; I'll be put'n in for a ranger job."

Chance just touched his hat and with a wave of his hand turned his horse towards Dallas, Craig and Katherine followed.

As he watched the three head out of town Riley sensed someone walking up to him. He looked over his shoulder and saw it was Brodie. Brodie was also watching the three ride out and said to Riley, "Well, I'll grab some boys and we can head on out to that camp and bury what's left of those outlaws. I know they was bad, but they need a Christian burial."

Riley looked at Brodie and smiling just shook his head, "Nope, you leave me out of it. I ain't bury'n none of 'em."

"Well, damn Riley, why not?"

"It's simple, Brodie. That big man draws a hard line, maybe the hardest, and, well, because some day Jed Chance may come back to town."

The rain began to fall.

Chapter 24

It was the night of the fifth day of travel for the trio. Travel had not proved difficult and Katherine had proven to be strong and resilient. Jed and Craig had seen that at times she could be caught staring off into the distance with tears in her eyes, undoubtedly thinking of her sister, Rose, but she would wipe the tears away and gather herself to move forward.

They had brought along some canvas to make her a shelter each night to provide her some privacy, but she insisted that Jed sleep just outside her tent. She would not go to sleep unless he assured her he would sleep close and keep watch over her.

Katherine had retired for the night and the two friends had banked the fire and each was smoking the last of their quirlies, sitting in silence, enjoying the peace of the night.

"Uh, Craig, I don't know for sure if I thanked you for—for what you did that night in that camp. You came through for me, just like I said you would, Pard. You saved my life and I surely do appreciate it. Surely do."

"Glad to do it, my friend. It needed doing and, well—I just did it and it didn't need any thinking on. I'm trying to deal with the war and all like we spoke on. I think I have 'bout got a handle on it. You know, trying to put it all in per—pro—"

"Perspective."

"Yea, that'll be it. Proper perspective and trying to move on with what we have in front of us like we need to get a plan on how we gon'a get the ranch laid out and—Well, 'course first me and Ruth is gon'a get hitched then we'll get that ranch laid out. Boy, I missed that woman something fierce. I think—"

"Craig, I got to get settled with Sam Rogers," interrupted Jed. "We ain't gon'a have no kind'a life trying to run a ranch and watch our backs looking out for that bastard."

"Jed, don't you think Sam done headed for the hills, or, like the barkeep said, New Mexico territory? Hell, his scalp will probably wind up on some Comanche war lance or some such. That is some rough territory 'tween here and New Mexi. Sam ain't a coward, but if he survives getting to New Mexi, I don't think he wants any part of you or risk coming back to this area."

Jed just stared at his friend for a moment and then putting out his smoke said, "Well, tell 'ya what, Craig. We get to Dallas we'll see what Sheriff Barkley and old Riley back in Lampas can scare up 'bout where Sam might be then we'll decide what to do. Turn in, Pard and get some sleep. I'll take first watch."

Jed watched his friend settle in for the night and then placed his saddle a few feet from Katherine's tent and settled down for his watch. His thoughts were on the ranch and Craig's dream of what could be, but Jed knew that he could not settle down to ranching with Sam Rogers and that Rio fella still above ground and kicking. He had made a promise to Rose and Mrs. Henderson and he intended to keep it. It wouldn't do to get Craig all riled up now but once they got back to Dallas and got their starter herd from Mrs. Henderson settled in, then he would have to let Craig know that he needed to find Sam and settle things.

Some two or so hours after Craig had settled down and with his snores helping to keep Jed awake, Katherine woke up. Jed could hear her rustling around in her tent and shortly she exited and looking over at him said, "Nature calls. I'll be back shortly." She moved off just into the brush and did what nature required and upon returning asked Jed, "Mind if I sit with you awhile?"

"No, Ma'am, you sit yourself down and enjoy the night."

The two sat in silence just enjoying the peace of it all. Jed watched the young girl and began to study, maybe for the first time, the lady that he and Craig had rescued. Tall for a woman, she was probably just seven or eight inches shorter than him and lean she was, with a very pleasing womanly shape. Her hair was as dark as the night and long. It hung to her mid back and thick, oh it was thick and right now a bit of a tangled mess, but she seemed unconcerned with it. He liked that. She turned to look at him and smiled. He thought of her and her face and even though the dark kept him from really seeing them, he remembered the green eyes, the scattering of freckles across her little, upturned nose and on her cheeks. All in all, she was a pretty woman and — why was this just registering on him now? He didn't know, and it made him a little uncomfortable to be thinking about her the way he was thinking.

"You ought to be getting some sleep, Miss. Katherine."

"Yes, but it's so nice out tonight. A clear sky, full moon, stars so bright. Jed, I know I told you before, but I just can't thank you enough for what you did, you and Craig. You saved me and it's just that—"

"Let's don't speak on it, Miss. Katherine. 'Sides, your grandma did offer us money to fetch you back—you and Rose, so—"

"That doesn't matter to me. The fact is, you saved me and if things had been different, maybe you could have saved Rose, but at least you got those that took us and killed my sweet sister. You did that, and I'm glad you did! They deserved everything you did to 'em and—"

"Whoa, Miss. Katherine, you're getting a little worked up and might wake old Craig up. My, I surely can tell you got Henderson blood in you, girl. You're as gritty as your grandma. I made a promise to your sister when we came on her. I promised her I would see to justice being done on them that—well—that harmed her. I been keeping that promise and I intend on finishing it too."

"Does that mean you'll be going after Sam Rogers?"

"Yes, it does. Soon as we can get a line on him and where he might be, I'll be going for him. The thing with Sam and I goes back to the war, not just what he did to you and Rose. During the war he killed a good woman, a nurse. He and his brothers raped and killed her, just like Rose. They stole medicine that was meant for the wounded too. I could only prove the stealing, not the other, but they did it. Sure as I'm sitting here, they did it."

They sat in silence for few minutes then turning to Jed, Katherine said, "I—I wished you wouldn't. I know Rose, and I know she would understand if you stayed—stayed in Dallas and just let it go. If—if something happened to you it would— I mean, I don't want anything to happen to you and I want to—to—"

"Miss. Katherine, it would eat at me if I just let it go. For me, that promise I made to Rose is—well, it's as close to a sacred kind of thing as I can do. I have to finish this. 'Sides, I don't reckon on spending my life worrying on if Sam Rogers just shows up and shoots me in the back and he is one that would be likely to do that."

"Ok, Jed, I guess I understand." Katherine stared off into the darkness for a moment but then, gathering her courage she shifted her body and moved closer to

Jed and took his hand.

"It's just that—well, Jed I was hoping that, well, you and I, when we get back to Dallas maybe we could—"

"What are you two chewing the dog over?" asked Craig, as he rose from his blankets. "Man can hardly sleep with all the yapping and such. 'Sides, I need to visit the bush." With that, Craig moved off to relieve himself.

Jed started at Katherine, and she, with all the confidence she could muster, stared right back at him.

Finally, he said, "Miss. Katherine, I don't rightly know what to say. I mean—"

Abruptly standing and turning toward her tent, Katherine said, "You think about it, Jed. You think about if maybe you and I could—well, court and just see where—just think on it!"

And with that, she entered her tent and after a few moments, Jed heard her settle down.

Upon returning to the now quiet camp Craig asked, "Well, I'm up, might as well sit the watch now so you can get some shut eye. Jed, are you hearing me?"

Snatched from his reverie by his friend's question, Jed said, "What—no. I mean no Pard, I ain't gon'a get no sleep tonight, and maybe not tomorrow night either. I got some thinking to do 'bout—well, 'bout things."

Smiling knowingly at his friend, mostly because he had heard the couple's conversation, Craig said, "Yep, bet you do at that. Well, friend, I'll be saying "good night" to 'ya and good luck with all that thinking and such." And with that Craig went back to his blankets and sleep, leaving his friend to ponder his future.

Chapter 25

It was the morning of the seventh day of travel. The trio was packed up and saddled and Jed was scattering the remnants of their breakfast fire when Craig approached him.

"Hey, Jed, I was just wondering on something."

"Yea, what might that be?"

"Well, I figure we will be making Dallas late today and well, I was wondering if you would mind if I just split off in a bit and head on to the ranch. Lordy! I miss that woman of mine and the boy so much and I just thought—"

"Sure thing, Craig, get yourself on over to 'em and I'll see to getting Katherine, I mean, Miss. Katherine on into Dallas and back with Mrs. Henderson."

"Good! If she goes ahead and settles with us just put my share with yours in the bank and I'll see you out at the ranch when you can make it and," smiling as he glanced over where Katherine was mounting her horse, and back at Jed, "Well, you just show up when you got things sorted out. I mean, Mrs. Henderson might not be too keen on Katherine hitched up to a thirty dollar a month man, but then again you did save Miss. Katherine and you do plan on being a big-time horse rancher and—"

"Pard, showing up to Ruth and the boy with a busted jaw just ain't no kind'a way to be showing up."

Craig slapped his friend on the back and said, "Just poking my friend, just fun'n."

Jed smiled, "I know Craig, me too. You plan on breaking off, I guess 'bout noon and head on to the ranch. You should make it, I guess, a couple of hours before we make Dallas. I'll see to settling with everything and get on home. Huh, listen to me, I already think of that old ranch as home. Anyway, I'll be on directly."

And so that's what they did. After breaking at noon, Craig said his goodbyes to the two but, not before Katherine gave him a big hug and a kiss on this check and thanked him for about the hundredth time for saving her and for the hundredth time Craig looked a little embarrassed and just mumbled a "you're welcome" or some such. Then he walked to where Jed was adjusting the saddle on his horse.

Craig pulled one of the Colts from its holster and stuck it in his waistband then unbuckled his gun belt and handing it to Jed he said to him, "Jed, I'll be keeping the shotgun, rifle and one of the handguns but, well, I don't need no rig like this, not no more, not ever again. Jed, I ain't like you. Hell, I don't reckon there is anyone else like you anywhere. I just want to be a rancher. I know Sam Rogers is still out there and I know you, but I can't hunt men nor kill no more. I'm done with it, my friend. I hope you can understand."

Jed listened to his friend then taking the rig from him and placing his hand on Craig's shoulder said, "You're a damn good man, Craig. Every man has to find his self and be true to his heart. I thank you for saving me back there in those woods and all the other times you had my back. You'll always be my friend. Hell, you're the only family I got."

Craig looked up at his friend and smiled. He offered his hand and the two men shook and with a nod Craig returned to horse and mounted up. He tipped his hat to Katherine, gave his friend a smile and a nod and headed for the ranch, leaving Jed and Katherine alone and with several hours of travel left in which they could discuss their feelings and future.

The two rode in silence for a while then Katherine said, "Jed, I want to talk. Now, don't say anything just yet, just let me get all this that has been crushing my insides, out. Now, we have known each other for all of almost two weeks and you know out here in the west a person has to sometimes act fast or lose out. Things happen quickly. My mom and dad being killed by Indians, my grandpa dying while trying to tame a bronc and, well, Rose, and all, shows me how a person just can't wait around on things. Now, I have feelings for you, strong feelings and not just because you saved me. Well, there may be some of that but it's more than that. I think I'm in love with you, least ways I am pretty sure I am, and I think —"

Jed, who had been listening with a growing discomfort interrupted, "Whoa, girl! Slow down a bit. I swear, you're going on like, well, you just be running on is all. Now, there are things 'bout me you don't know but you should know 'fore you go setting your sights on a no account like me. First— "

"You were born in Atlanta, Georgia, your father was some plantation owner, your mother — well, your mother was a lady of the night. She — she was," Katherine looked away for a moment then turned a steady

189

gaze back on Jed, "she was killed by a customer."

Jed looked on at Katherine, trying not to get lost in her green eyes and finally asked her, "How'd you know all that? I mean, we—oh, Craig, my good friend Craig done run his mouth! When I see him I'm gon'a—"

"Do nothing. He is your friend, your family even. I asked and he told me. Craig is smart and he could tell I was—well, developing feeling toward you. He wanted me to know about you. I'm sure he told me to see what kind of person I am and if any of that would make a difference to me. And I can tell you if it had, he would have shucked me like summer corn."

"What?"

"Never mind, I just mean that he had your best interest at heart and was just trying to protect you. Now, I am not asking you to decide something about us right now, just think on it and let's see, when we get to Dallas—"

"Yea, when we get to Dallas," Jed interrupted, "When we get there your grandma is gon'a be hiding you out at that ranch and will dare me to show my sorry face there. 'Sides, I got ten years on you, girl!"

"Frog lips!"

"Wha—what's that mean?"

"It means that is ridiculous. I don't care about that. It is foolishness is all. My momma was eleven years younger than my dad. Grandma, she was all of fourteen years younger than my grandpa when they married. But, I am not saying we are going to marry! I'm just saying let's visit and you court me and, well, we'll see."

"Miss. Katherine, I don't know now, maybe—"

"Damn you, Jed! It's Katherine, not Miss. Katherine! I could be making this offer to a bunch of other men and they would jump at the chance, but you—you may be fast as lightening with a gun and strong as any five men combined but dang if you aren't mule stubborn and slow on this!"

With that, Katherine tossed her long, ebony tresses and spurred her horse on toward Dallas. Jed followed along, trotting just behind her and lost in thought but also enjoying the view. She sure knew how to sit a saddle.

Three hours later, some miles to the North West, Craig Mullins reigned in his horse on a hill in sight of his ranch. All he could think of was how good it was to be home. He was home to Ruth and the boy. He could see smoke curling from the chimney, welcoming him home. Jed would be returning to the ranch tomorrow or the next day and they could begin making their dreams a reality, and he was going to marry Ruth. With that thought in mind, he spurred his horse on to the ranch and his family.

A few hours later, Katherine and Jed arrived in Dallas.

Chapter 26

Katherine and Jed rode slowly into Dallas. At first no one took notice but then Gibbs, the telegraph operator, spotted them.

"Yee Haw!! They're back! Somebody go fetch Mrs. Henderson! Her girl is back!"

By the time they made it to the sheriff's office they had quite a crowd following along yelling "welcome home" to Katherine and "Congratulations" or "Good job" to Jed. They both nodded politely in acknowledgment.

They reined in at Sheriff Barkley's office and found Barkley, his deputies, Bev and Tom Scott, and the Mayor, Henry Envoy, waiting and all with big smiles on their faces. They stepped off the porch as one as the two riders pulled up and dismounted.

"Damn Jed! Man, I didn't think there was any hope. I thought—well, to hell with what I thought. Damn good to see you man, damn good!" said Sheriff Barkley. Then turning to Katherine and tipping his hat, "Katherine, it's so good to see you, girl! Someone's gone to get your grandma from over at the hotel, so she should be along directly. I — we — well, so sorry 'bout Rose. It — "

Katherine cut the sheriff off, "Thanks, Sheriff Barkley thanks a lot. It's great to be home. If it wasn't for — "

Katherine didn't finish her sentence because the crowd suddenly parted and there was her grandma, Mrs. Henderson, her foreman, Luke Davis, and a score of the ranch's punchers. Tears of joy and grief sparkled in her grandma's eyes and flowed down her cheeks. The two women looked at each other for a moment then fell into each other's arms weeping and sharing words of love and their sorrow over Rose. The crowd that had gathered was jubilant and sounded words of welcome to both Katherine and Jed. By this time word had spread to Camp Street of the rescue and return of one of their own and celebratory gunshots could be heard.

Turning to his Deputies, Sheriff Barkley instructed them to go to Camp Street and restore order before someone was shot.

During all the tumult Jed had just stood by

watching and wishing Craig was with him to see all the doings.

Mrs. Henderson turned to Jed and for a moment just stared at the big man. Then, with tears flowing anew she took both his hands in hers.

"Jed, oh Jed, I can't begin to tell you how grate-ful—how thankful I am to you and Mr. Mullins for bringing home my Katherine. I am so very thankful. Thank you, thank you so much, Jed! Where is Mr. Mul-lins? Is he—?"

Jed was embarrassed by all the attention and re-moving one of his hands from her grasp, he removed his hat and speaking low said, "Craig is just fine, he just wanted to get on to the ranch to see Ruth and his boy is all. And you're welcome, Mrs. Henderson. Craig and I are just sorry 'bout Rose. We just didn't get there in time for her. We—"

"It's alright, Jed. You did more than most men could do. We will be forever in your debt."

During this time, Katherine had been standing just behind her grandma and she was smiling at Jed. There was her smile and a look in her eyes, and both held a lot of promise.

Mrs. Henderson said, "Jed, about that promise

you made, if—"

"It was kept, Mrs. Henderson. At least, best I could keep it. All but two of the men that took the girls are dead and none of them buried, least ways, not by us."

Turning to Sheriff Barkley he said, "Sheriff, they got most of the money off them outlaws and I think that bank in Lampasas is gon'a get it back to Dallas."

"Yep, they've been in touch 'bout getting it back, Jed. Bev knows that state policeman, Riley, and they swapped a few telegraphs with Riley telling what you did. The way he told it, well, it was unbelievable what you did, but I'd like to know what—"

"Hold on Sheriff," interrupted Mrs. Henderson, "I'm going to take Katherine to the hotel to get washed up and get some rest. You men can do all your talking but meet us there for dinner 'bout eight. Jed, there's a room for you at the hotel just ask for the key. We'll see you at eight for supper and we'll discuss getting settled on those horses. I have already put four thousand dollars in the bank under the names of Jed Chance and Craig Mullins so you can get to spending when you want. I put it in there the day you two left Dallas. I had a good feeling." The old woman smiled and winked at Jed.

With that, Katherine and Mrs. Henderson headed for the hotel while the men, as many as could, followed Jed into the Sheriff's office to hear about what had happened during the chase for the outlaws and girls.

At dinner that night, Mrs. Henderson told Jed that she had already sent men to her ranch to get the two stallions and the mares she had picked out for Jed and Craig and to start moving them to their ranch.

"They're good stock, Jed, some of my best. I know you both will be pleased. I hope you would trust that I would do right by you and Craig with the horses I picked out. I had them cut from my herd when I learned you were all in Lampasas. I did straight by you both, I promise. Right after you and Craig left out to fetch the girls, I took the liberty of having some of the boys go out to your ranch and build a couple of corrals and I went along to tell Ruth what was going on. It wouldn't do to have your horses wondering all over Texas. Always remain positive, Jed. That's what I believe. I knew you two would—well, I thought things would turn out ok, and they turned out as well as we could have hoped, I guess."

"You got no truck with me, Mrs. Henderson. I trust your word and your eye for horse flesh. That mare you picked for me is a great horse and I am most happy with her. I know you have picked us out some good ones for the ranch."

During supper there was not much time for Jed and Katherine to talk but they exchanged a lot of lingering glances, a fact that was not lost on Mrs. Henderson. Later, when Jed went out on the porch of the hotel and was rolling a smoke Mrs. Henderson joined him there.

"Jed, I am just going to get straight to the point. I am too old to banter about. Katherine has told me about her — well, her feeling toward you and she thinks that those feelings may be returned in kind. Now, don't interrupt an old woman, let me finish. I know that what Katherine feels may be just a profound sense of gratefulness, but I also know that my girls — I mean, Katherine, is not fool-headed. So, if you are so inclined towards her and you two want to explore a possible future together, well, I won't stand in the way. She could do worse and lord knows I don't know if she could find a better man."

"Mrs. Henderson, I am most appreciative, I surely am and, well, might be that we do have feelings for each other. I guess, well, I guess we'll just ride things along and see what happens, but there is something else we have to speak on." Jed stood up from where he had been sitting on the porch rail and looked off into the night and said, "It's not over between Sam Rogers and me. I killed his two brothers and he lives by the law of the feud. One day he'll be coming for me. So, I have to decide if I am going to wait on him, or take the fight to him instead. I have to decide and right soon."

"OK, Jed we'll just see how it plays out. By the way, Katherine and I are going to ride out to your ranch with you in the morning to pay our respects to Craig and his family. My—I mean, your horses should be there by then and you and Craig can look them over and if you aren't pleased with any of them I'll have my men take them back and you two can ride over and pick out replacements for them. How's that sound?"

"Sounds fine, Mrs. Henderson, now if you don't mind, I'm going to turn in. I will see you ladies in the morning for breakfast. Good night, and please tell Katherine I said good night."

"Good night, Jed. We'll see you in the morning."

Morning came and the three had breakfast together, then, accompanied by Mrs. Henderson's foreman, Luke Davis, and two other ranch hands, they headed for Craig and Jed's ranch. They had crossed the Trinity and were almost within eyesight of the ranch when they saw the rider coming. He was coming from the direction of the ranch, and he was coming hard.

Chapter 27

At the sight of the rider coming at them, a feeling of dread settled over Jed. He loosened the Colt in his cross-draw holster and moved his horse across the face of the mounts of Katherine and Mrs. Henderson, offering some protection to them. No one spoke; they just watched the rider coming until finally Luke said, "Its ok, that's Thomas coming. He's one of our boys, but man he is riding hard!"

It seemed that the rider just noticed their party and he angled his pony to head toward them. In another few moments, he arrived and reigned in hard, his pony snorting and panting.

"Luke, Mrs. Henderson, better come quick! It's terrible, these folks, they are—come quick, now!"

With dread filling his heart, Jed spurred his big horse toward the ranch. It wasn't long before the party came in sight of the ranch. The horses that Mrs. Henderson had sent to the ranch were grazing in the corrals that had been built to the right of the barn. Four men stood huddled together outside the barn, hats in their hands, talking. That was the scene as Jed and the rest thundered into the ranch yard. Jed's horse had not come to a full stop before he was out of the saddle and walking toward the men.

Jed was afraid for his friends, but he was trying to remain calm. "Where's Craig? Where are they?" He asked.

Luke was off his horse almost as fast as Jed and quickly caught up with him.

"It's ok boys, this here is Jed Chance, and this is his ranch too."

One of the ranch hands, hat in his hand, turned to Jed and spoke, "Mister, the folks at this ranch done been murdered. I'm sorry, but that's the short of it. One of 'em is over in the barn, the others — "

Jed struck out toward the barn before the man could finish, anger and sorrow beginning to build in him. The other men struggled to keep up.

Jed pushed the barn door but already smelled death before it opened. There on the ground was, Jeff. Looking at his bloated body, Jed could see knife wounds on his arms and chest, but it appeared he had died from a gunshot to the head as most of the top of his head was gone. He had been dead for several days.

Without speaking, Jed turned and headed for the ranch house. As he was crossing the yard, he passed Mrs. Henderson and Katherine who were talking with the men who had found the bodies. Katherine stepped in front of Jed, trying to block his way.

"Jed! Jed, don't go in there! Please, Jed, they told me what—"

Without speaking, Jed easily stepped around her and continued toward the house with Luke and several other ranch hands in tow, trying to keep up.

Mrs. Henderson put her hand on her granddaughter's shoulder and spoke gently to her, "Leave him be. He has to do it and I pity anyone that tries to stop him."

Jed stepped on the porch and immediately his nose was filled with the stink of death. He stopped for a moment, staring at the door. He knew already what he would find in the house. He knew, but had to go thru that door and face it. Even as his hand pushed the door open, he was filled with sorrow for his friend and his family.

Craig was on his back on the floor of the house.

The charred remains of his feet and lower legs were in the now cold fireplace. His arms were spread out and his hands had been nailed to the floor of the ranch house. He was shirtless and large cuts covered his chest. The cuts the doctor had sewn up were pulled open. A large pool of almost dried blood was under his head, the results of his throat being cut from ear to ear and so deep that his head was barely attached to his body.

A huge sigh escaped Jed and his big body seem to slump. The men standing behind him later reported that they thought they heard a low moan, but no one was sure.

Jed stared at his friend's violated body for several moments. The men behind him did not move or speak. Jed then walked slowly to the bedroom. Ruth was lying on the bed. She was naked, and her legs and arms had been tied to the bed posts. It appeared she had been dead for a couple of days and her body was beginning to swell from the onset of decomposition, but it was evident that death had not come easily or quickly for her.

The men of the Henderson ranch were all hard and capable men. Most had fought Indians and bad men, and some had served in the war. None of them were strangers to death, but for most of those that had entered the cabin, the scene of carnage and brutality was too much. Several hurried from that place of death out into the sunlight. One of the men went to his horse, mounted and rode away, never to be heard from again. All of them were profoundly changed by what they had seen.

Jed turned to the remaining men in the cabin, "I'll be asking you all to leave now. Leave me for a bit with my friend and his—his wife."

The men turned and left the cabin.

Out on the porch Luke encountered Katherine. She had been contemplating going into the house, but Luke placed his hand on her arm and just shook his head. All he could say with a voice that was choked was, "Don't. Don't go in there, Miss. Katherine. What's in there, well it ain't fit for no woman to see and fact is, no man nether."

Luke told one of the men to go to Dallas and bring back the Sheriff.

Luke spoke to no one in particular when he said, "Someone get something to get those nails out of Craig's hands."

When Katherine and Mrs. Henderson heard

those words they both paled and after a moment Katherine took her grandmother by the arm and they moved off to stand by the horses.

Moments later someone handed Luke a smithy's puller that had been found in the barn.

About thirty or so minutes after being left alone with Craig to mourn his passing and that of his lady, Jed came out on the porch. He saw the pullers in Luke's hand and took them while asking, "Luke, you got anybody that can track?"

"Well, yeah, that long-haired fellow over by the corral. He's part Apache and he's a hell of a tracker. He was a scout for the Calvary till he took an arrow to the knee. That slowed him down a might."

"See if he can cut some sign. I want to know how many and where they went. I already know who. And Luke, get some of the boys to prepare a place for em, please," said Jed.

"Sure, Jed, we'll get right on it."

Luke set about doing what Jed had asked while Jed went inside to pull the nails from his friend's hands.

Jed had just finished with his grim task when he heard Mrs. Henderson calling from the porch. Jed went outside where he found Mrs. Henderson and Katherine standing together.

"Jed, listen to me. I know it's bad in there, but these old eyes have seen men dead and dying. I buried my husband after he had been crushed by a wild horse, and my son and his wife when both had been scalped and their bodies desecrated by Indians. I know things are — well, things are bad in there, but Katherine and I can handle it. You see to Craig, we'll take care of Ruth. Please, Jed, I need to do this for them, both of them."

Seeing the look of purpose and determination on both women's faces, Jed relented but not before asking Katherine, "Are you sure you want to go in there?"

Swallowing hard but with steel in her voice, Katherine responded. "Yes, I am. Jed. Craig helped save my life. It's the least I can do for him, and his."

Jed just nodded and turned and walked back into the ranch house with the women close behind. Jed tried to block the view of Craig's body, but the women saw enough that both gave a sharp intake of breath as they quickly turned their heads and entered the bedroom. A moment later Katherine came out, and turning her eyes away from the horror on the floor, and with a voice choked with emotion, she asked Jed for his knife, so they could cut the bindings from Ruth's arms and legs. A moment later, Mrs. Henderson went back outside and found a water bucket next to the trough and when she began to use the brand-new water pump she thought back to the day she had approached Craig and Jed about rescuing her girls and how Craig had asked for the new pump to help his woman and boy. She remembered watching her men installing the new pump and the gratefulness that Ruth showed, along with the fear she had for her man's safety. She could not help feeling at least partly responsible for what had happened to Ruth and Craig. Tears filled her eyes and for a moment she wavered on going back into the house, but she steeled herself and went back. She and Katherine, ignoring the smell, washed Ruth's body and wrapped her in a sheet for burial.

Jed cleaned Craig as best he could and wrapped him in a blanket. About a hundred yards or so west and north of the ranch house there was a stand of four oaks. There, Luke and the others had dug three graves. Jed carried Craig to his grave first, then Ruth, then went to the barn and cleaned Jeff up and wrapped him in a blanket and took him and laid him in his grave.

Mrs. Henderson spoke words over the graves of the three, but Jed didn't really hear much of what she said. He was focused on his loss of family and the unquenchable thirst for vengeance that had taken firm root in his heart.

Several hours after the three had been laid to rest Luke approached Jed who was with Katherine and Mrs. Henderson sitting next to the barn. They had mutually agreed to stay at the ranch until the sheriff showed up.

"Jed, my man cut sign for you. Two riders headed out north but once they hit a rocky area 'bout three miles away they headed west, moving fast. Jed, there's something else. One of the men found this tacked to the barn when they first rode in and it has your name on it."

Luke handed Jed a tattered piece of paper. It was a note.

Jed read;

"**who ever finds this here note, get it to Jed bastard Chance. He kiled my brothers. Jed I kiled Craig and his famly like you kiled mine. We had a migt of fun with his woman while we was loking for you two to git here but just Craig showed up. He said you was gone to New Mexi looking for me. I swear, no mount of working on that boy got him to say differnt so I gess he wernt lying. I be heded there for you and me to settle up.**"

Sam

Rising from where he had been sitting against the barn wall and adjusting his gun belt, Jed said, "Yea, well, I reckoned they would eventually head west. It was Sam Rogers and that Rio fella that's riding with 'em. They'll be the last two left of the gang that took Rose and Katherine."

Jed read the note once more then folded it up and put it in his pocket.

"You heading out after 'em?" asked Luke.

"Oh yeah, I'll be going out to kill them two, but I'll take my time. They'll be looking for me and be all watchful like. Time will pass, and they'll get less watchful and careless, a little. Then when they ain't thinking 'bout me, I'll be there, and I'll settle it all for Craig and his family and Rose too. First, though, I got something to do for Mrs. Henderson, and then I'll be going."

Chapter 28

Winter was coming on and the rising sun made the frost on the buffalo grass sparkle as it swayed in the gentle morning breeze. The riders advancing on the grove of pecan and oak trees cast long shadows. Jed and Katherine were side by side, leading the wagon containing Mrs. Henderson, a driver, and a coffin, made special in Dallas. There were six heavily armed outriders, three to a side and twenty yards out, riding in silence except for the creak of saddle leather and the occasional snort of a horse.

The party had arrived the day before, late in the afternoon, but Mrs. Henderson didn't want to go to Rose at night, she wanted to wait until morning, so they had camped some distance from the grove.

"Kate, you sure you want to go in there?" asked Jed.

"Yes, Jed, I have to do it. It—just like you had to go into Craig's house, I have to face this so I can move on."

At the mention of his friend Jed looked quickly away, toward the south. Katherine knew that Jed's blue eyes were probably blinking back tears. It had been a little more than a month since the discovery of the bodies of his friends and it had been a tough time for Jed. Mrs. Henderson had insisted that he move out to their ranch and there he and Katherine had grown closer and they knew that there was love between them, but they both knew that before there would be anything more, Jed had a score to settle. A week or so after burying his friends, Jed had returned to Craig's ranch with Katherine and the two of them burned the ranch to the ground. They had mutually decided that no one should ever again live in that place that had seen the horrors that had been committed there.

The party pulled up just outside the grove and dismounted. Jed helped Mrs. Henderson down from the wagon.

I'll take you to her."

She just nodded and taking him by the arm and Katherine by the hand they moved into the grove, leaving the others to keep watch.

The leaves were turning to their red and gold

colors and were falling from the trees creating a carpet for the three to walk on. Katherine only momentarily hesitated at the spot where she had been tied and where she had listened to the horrors being forced on her sister. Jed made no mention of nor did he point out the spot where he found Rose's body, he just led the ladies unerringly to where he and Craig had laid Rose to rest.

He led the ladies through the last stand of brush and there was Rose's grave. Jed removed the black, low brim hat he was wearing. Their movements startled a hawk that had been perched in the Oak tree that stood at the end of the arm of land where Rose lay and the big bird screamed in protest as he took flight. Rose's grave was undisturbed. The three stopped and after a moment, Mrs. Henderson walked to Rose's grave and kneeling she placed both hands on the dark and smooth river rocks that covered her and bowed her head. Katherine moved to her grandmother and placed a hand on her shoulder.

"Uh, Mrs. Henderson, Kate, I'm gon'a move back a bit and have a smoke. When you're ready, just call and I'll go fetch some of the boys with the casket, but—take your time."

With that, Jed backed off into the brush, giving

the women time to mourn anew their loved one. Jed rolled a quirley and thought about all that had happened since he had arrived in Dallas and about what he had left to do. Shortly after finding the horrors at the ranch, Mrs. Henderson had written the new governor, a friend of her deceased husband, about appointing Jed a Texas Ranger but she had not heard back from him. With or without the ranger appointment, he was going after the men that had killed his friends.

Jed had been waiting about thirty minutes when he heard Katherine calling for him and he went to her and Mrs. Henderson.

"I'll go get the boys and —"

"No, Jed. She'll rest here. It's a good place. It's peaceful and, well, if I had to choose a place to rest, I couldn't do better than right here," said Mrs. Henderson. Her tear streaked face looked up at Jed and smiled. "Might be, when the time comes, you'd like to rest here."

Returning her smile Jed replied, "Well, long as it ain't too soon," and looking at Katherine, "and if, well, if —"

"Yes, well, I think there's room here for you and Katherine to keep Rose company."

"Don't rush it, Jed, just don't rush it!" said Katherine as she gave him a slight smile.

The three looked at each other and smiled and with a last parting look at Rose's grave, they went back to where the others were waiting.

Arriving back at the wagon, Mrs. Henderson called out to one of her riders, "Paul! Paul, have you got that map?"

One of the outriders galloped up and dismounted. He dug into his saddle bag and pulled out a map which he opened and spread out on the rear of the wagon. Bending over the map Mrs. Henderson asked, "Ok Paul, where on this map are we?"

Paul, who had spent years scouting the area for the army placed his finger on the map and said, "Here, Mrs. Henderson. We are here next to this stream. It's a pretty good ride to anywhere from this spot."

"Doesn't matter to me," she said. Then taking her finger, she drew a large circle on the map that placed the area of Rose's grave in the center, "I'm claiming all of this land here. We'll get it staked and do what has to be done but I'm putting a claim on it, now. Rose won't be among strangers."

Several hours later, after eating a meal, the group prepared to begin the journey back to Dallas, save one.

Katherine stood by Jed as he cinched up his big, black horse.

"Jed, I know you have to do this, but please, please be careful."

"Careful as I can, Kate, promise."

The two stood and stared at each other, and then, taking Katherine by the shoulders, Jed said, "You know, I never did get around to naming this here horse," he said as he smiled at Katherine, "but I think I've decided to name her, 'Kate'. What do you think?"

Katherine laughed and reaching up, she placed a kiss on his lips, "Yes, 'Kate' is a fine name for such a pretty horse. I like it. Now, each time you talk to her you will be saying my name. It will be a reminder."

"I don't need that name to remind me of you. If—"

Jed didn't finish the sentence because at that moment Mrs. Henderson walked up accompanied by one of her hands, leading Jed's pack horse. Jed took the reins of the horse and trailed them.

"Jed, you take care. You find those men; kill 'em and get back home. We'll mind your horses for you 'til you get back. If you need anything, anything at all you get in touch. Kate, honey, we got to go." With that, she returned to the wagon where one of her hands helped her up.

Jed walked Kate to her horse. She turned and looked at him with tears shining in her eyes. She didn't trust herself to say much so she just said, "Please, mount and go. I can't leave here with you still looking at me."

Jed placed his big hand gently on her cheek and kissed her.

"I'll be back, Kate. Trust me on that. I'll be back."

With that, Jed returned to his horse, took up the reins to the pack horse and mounted up. He turned and giving Kate one last look spurred his horse and moved off south.

The Henderson party moved off toward Dallas. After a few moments, Mrs. Henderson turned and saw Kate, mounted on her horse, just sitting there, watching Jed riding south, toward Lampasas.

"Paul, you and one other stay here with Kate. Lord knows she'll be watching him for as long as she can see him. When she's done, ya'll bring her along, please."

"We'll do, Mrs. Henderson."

Kate watched Jed riding south for as long as her eyes could see him and then some.

For his part, Jed struggled with leaving Kate,

but he knew what he had to do. As soon as he turned his horse's head south and put spurs to her his heart hardened and he allowed the rage that he had felt since Craig's death flow through his body. He was set on killing Sam Rogers and the man called Rio and heaven help anyone who got in his way.